The Courage of One

The Courage of ONE

A NOVEL

Marion Hendricks

THE COURAGE OF ONE

iUniverse books may be ordered through booksellers or by contacting:

iUniverse
1663 Liberty Drive
Bloomington, IN 47403
www.iuniverse.com
1-800-Authors (1-800-288-4677)

Because of the dynamic nature of the Internet, any web addresses or links contained in this book may have changed since publication and may no longer be valid. The views expressed in this work are solely those of the author and do not necessarily reflect the views of the publisher, and the publisher hereby disclaims any responsibility for them.

Any people depicted in stock imagery provided by Thinkstock are models, and such images are being used for illustrative purposes only.
Certain stock imagery © Thinkstock.

ISBN: 978-1-4917-7166-2 (sc)
ISBN: 978-1-4917-7165-5 (e)

Library of Congress Control Number: 2015912399

Print information available on the last page.

iUniverse rev. date: 08/25/2015

In loving memory of my beloved parents, Michael and Kathleen,
and with deep gratitude to my brothers and
sisters and their respective families
for their encouragement and belief in me.

CHAPTER 1

"Alex, come and help me with this cupboard, please!" Marcia called from her bedroom window.

Why can't my sister leave me to do one job at a time? Alex thought. *I still have to rake up these leaves, Dad wants me to scrub the conservatory roof, and very soon Mum will be calling me to help her with the shopping.*

"Alex, hurry, we'll be leaving in an hour – and no sunglasses, please!" Michaela yelled.

"But, *Mum—*"

"I mean it, Alex! You can barely see through them. Last week you wanted me to carry two of the bags after you met your coach in the store. Remember?" Michaela and Marcia, her eldest, smiled at Alex's feigned indignation.

"Yes, because he remarked on the way I was dressed and told me I'm not a ox. He said I needed to take more care of my body and stop lifting or carrying heavy things," Alex responded ingenuously while pulling on a baseball cap.

"*An* ox," she corrected. "And by the way, he's not your mother, *I* am! He's far too nosey, that one!"

Alex helped Marcia with her cupboard. Then he washed down the conservatory roof and emptied the kitchen bin before presenting himself with a spruced-up look, all ready for the weekly shopping. They all heard the sound of Alex's teammates, the budding cricket stars, approaching. Marcia and her mother smiled pleasantly when they recognized the familiar voices.

The boys were flipping a coin to decide which of them would play on the same team as Alex; there was no better cricket player. They ran when they saw Alex in the driveway, for they had strict instructions from the older players to ensure there'd be more weekend matches with Alex to improve their chances of beating the other teams.

"What about a few matches today, mate?" one of the boys asked Alex as the group reached the family car.

"I played until three, while you were doing chores. I'm going out now. See ya!" Alex shot back.

"But we were told not to come without you," they informed Alex, rattling off the names of the other team members who had so instructed them. "They reckon we won't be able to beat the school teams without you."

"Sorry, mate. I told you *my* Saturdays are as unpredictable as the weather. Play without me."

"What about a lift to the cricket field, boys?" Alex's mother said as she reversed the Polo from the garage.

"Thanks, Mrs Versini," one of the boys replied tentatively. "Uh, could Alex come and play after the shopping?"

"Of course. Hop in! We should be back in time for at least one or two matches."

The boys were thrilled as they loaded their cricket ball, bat, wickets, stumps, and bails into the luggage compartment before sliding into the backseat, and they were smiling broadly.

Alex felt awkward about the arrangement between his mother and the boys. They were unaware of their friend's preliminary routine prior to any game: chest-strapping, rubber bands placed around socks, stuffing cricket boots, positioning the baseball cap and the regular gloves he wore under leather ones borrowed from Dad's collection. *Nobody really cares about me,* Alex thought, brushing away angry tears.

Despite being the youngest, Alex was not spared the most menial tasks. Whereas his older sisters spent their time and energy doing assignments or weekend jobs, Alex was dubbed "Mum's right hand", and Michaela relied on him for the unexpected tasks in the home.

The family generally admired their relationship and considered it cute whenever Alex called their mother "Michaela" instead of "Mum" to emphasize a point or to secure special privileges.

CHAPTER 2

"**W**hat was that delay in the bathroom about, Alex?" Michaela asked. "Dad says you're taking far too long these days. In any case, we will need some of the dry wood from the garage – we're having a barbecue this evening. Will you chop some, please?" Then she set about making herself a cup of tea.

"Michaela!" Alex exclaimed. "Could my beloved sisters not lift their darling bottoms for a change, especially with tonight's barbecue? All they do is parade in new clothes, blow-dry their hair, and paint their toenails."

"Quiet, Alex. I don't want your dad to hear you. You know how angry he gets when you raise your voice like that."

"That's right – *my* needs and feelings *don't* count. As long as I'm kept busy ..." Alex's voice quivered with emotion.

"Shhh! Keep your voice down; he's in the lounge," she said as she returned to plant a kiss on the top of Alex's head. "Of course you have needs, honey. As for your sisters, they *will* do their share.

"Girls!" she called out, "we need you to arrange the patio seating and tableware, please!" The twins, three years older than Alex, were clearly their dad's favourite daughters. This did not deter Michaela from ensuring that they did their fair share of chores in the home. She had a special appreciation for Alex, their seventh and last born. He had been relied upon from an early age to do even the toughest jobs without the slightest murmur.

Alex followed Michaela to the garage, and together they set up the barbecue stand with wood, coal, and tongs, ready for Brigido to take charge of the cookout. She liked to boast to her

3

friends about her husband, who usually ensured that the meat was well cooked.

The four older girls were in the kitchen marinating the meat and preparing the salads.

"Michaela, I'd like to spend my summer holidays with Nan and Grandpa," Alex requested when they were alone. "I need a good holiday and time to sort myself out."

"What's brought this on, Alex?"

"Oh, Michaela, you guys really need to make up your minds. First you preach, 'Your poor Nan and Grandpa are missing you', and now you ask, 'What's brought this on, Alex?'"

Alex had a way of mimicking Michaela, and it never failed to amuse her.

Michaela smiled and chucked Alex's chin affectionately on her way to answer the front door.

"Good afternoon, Father," Michaela said. "Brigido's about halfway with the barbecue. Come and join us for drinks and snacks in the meantime. But if it's something urgent, Alex can fall in and do the job for Brigido."

"Let him carry on, Michaela, and thanks – I'll take up your offer and enjoy a drink."

Brigido usually met with Fr Paulino once a month to assist with the parish financial records and banking. But when the priest appeared at their family barbecue, seated with Michaela and his six daughters in the courtyard, Brigido felt uneasy. Though the family appeared naturally warm and friendly, Fr Paulino barely made eye contact with him. As well, his much-loved youngest child, Alex, seemed tense.

"What's happening here, Father? Not a conspiracy of sorts, is it?" Brigido was half amused and spoke just above a whisper while the girls were serving their supper.

Marcia looked at Brigido, and as was typical of his eldest daughter, she gave him a glass of cool water and reminded him that Fr Paulino had been invited.

Fr Paulino informed Brigido that this meeting had been prearranged by a family member. He encouraged Brigido to relax and first listen before he jumped to any conclusions. He was meant to act as a facilitator and not a family counsellor.

"*Facilitator?*" Brigido said incredulously. "Who authorized you to sort out problems in this house?"

"Who spoke about problems? Like I said, I've been asked," Fr Paulino said, mopping his brow with his immaculate handkerchief. "The sooner you give me a chance to speak, the better."

"If I cannot trust my family, what's the use?"

Again Fr Paulino gently informed him that there was something a member of the family wanted everyone to hear.

"But we discussed impending family events days ago – we usually mull over matters like clothes, pocket money, air time, anything – so what's all this about?"

"Calm down, Brigido. There is a matter that you haven't spoken about for years, and maybe it's time you did. And you need not be defensive, my good man. Just listen. You'll get your chance!"

"Do I have a family of traitors who go behind my back to the priest instead of facing me? Who put you up to this?" he demanded. The tension reduced Michaela and their daughters to silence.

At the sound of the doorbell, one of the girls got up to answer it. Their paternal grandmother, accompanied by a well-dressed gentleman, greeted each family member in a warm and caring manner. Then she invited the gentleman to speak.

"I am Gerald, the cricket coach, and I'm here to tell you that I am no longer able to accept Alex as part of our cricket club – an excellent player, no doubt – but no longer eligible!"

"What has Alex done?" Brigido asked, balling his fists. "If it's theft or bad company, there's nothing a good hiding cannot fix. But taking Alex out of the team and coming all this way to tell me is cowardly, loathsome, and downright low!"

Brigido's mother admonished him gently while rubbing his arm. She pleaded with him to listen to Gerald without jumping to conclusions. She assured him that there was not a single complaint about Alex.

"I know, Ma, but Alex is a *top* player. They have their favourites, that's all!"

Gerald spoke in an even tone. "Mr Versini, Alex is not only our *favourite* player but the *best*, and therefore this decision was made with absolute fairness."

"*Fairness?* What do *you* know about being fair?" Brigido demanded.

"I've said my piece, and with respect, I must add that this is in Alex's best interest."

"Says *who*?" Brigido hollered. "Who appointed *you* to decide what's best for my child?" That was when his mother divulged that *she* had initiated this meeting. After listening to Alex, she had set the wheels in motion to put a stop to all the drama in Alex's life.

"Alex's life? What do you mean, Ma?" Brigido's voice was considerably louder as he addressed his mother. "If there's something you're trying to tell me, Ma, please do so. Stop beating about the bush. I've had a heavy day today. I don't need this …" His voice cracked.

The girls appeared full of tension, so Michaela signalled them to organize tea for everyone while she followed the conversation between Brigido and his mother.

By the time they were ready for tea, Michaela's tear-stained cheeks revealed that there was still some unfinished business. Marcia proposed that she and her sisters be included in further talks and asked Fr Paulino to facilitate their deliberations. They were old enough to have their say, she told them.

Brigido listened attentively to Gerald as he explained his rationale for dropping Alex from the team but made no response. Marcia, however, apologized to Gerald for her dad's arrogance and thanked him for the courageous stand he had taken. Fr Paulino appeared shaken by Brigido's stubbornness and was unwilling to pursue the matter any further.

Gerald and Fr Paulino departed on a cordial note, leaving Michaela and her daughters feeling bewildered, embarrassed, and utterly helpless.

CHAPTER 3

The family gathered while the twins were at the youth club to discuss their forthcoming sixteenth birthday. Michaela and Brigido were excited about this huge event – the twins had been their pride and joy from the day they were born – and no expense would be spared. They planned to make this the biggest birthday event the family had ever seen; the girls would have a day to remember. The siblings promised to lend a hand without revealing the plans to them.

In the upmarket area the family had moved to, a family barbecue was considered highly unsuitable for celebrating birthdays. Not classy enough, it seemed. The girls were particularly ecstatic about the prospect of new outfits for such occasions. Their parents could never do enough for their dear daughters, who epitomized affection, joy, and goodwill. Therefore, every birthday was celebrated in style.

Marcia and her sisters were tasked with arranging the video camera to capture the surprise elements and spontaneity of the celebration. Though up to five years apart, the sisters shared the same colouring of jet-black hair and violet eyes, and there was a special bond among them. They moved in the same circles – often being mistaken for three sets of twins – with Marcia as their spokeswoman.

Maria, the second eldest, offered to use photographs from the family album and get started on a PowerPoint presentation with catchy quotes of the twins' first words, their respective stages, their fantasy games caught on camera, and some ridiculously funny anecdotes that their parents recounted. Her plan was to present this to family and guests while they enjoyed drinks and canapés. In addition, each sister enthusiastically agreed to prepare a special birthday wish for the twins.

7

Marcia volunteered to facilitate the catering, while their dad promised to do all the driving before and after the party. Alex would assist with the hired glassware, crockery and cutlery, monogrammed serviettes, and the birthday cake.

When Brigido met Michaela's eyes, it made him remember Gerald Fredericks. He was even more determined to involve Alex as fully as possible. Brigido was a good husband, but Michaela realized they would eventually have to talk about Alex. It was a sore point between them, but it was high time they did something constructive. Maybe when Alex was a bit older and more open to change? Time would tell.

Michaela discussed the décor, colour scheme, girls' outfits, and shopping arrangements with her four daughters, but none of them ventured to voice their undisclosed question: "What about Alex?"

———❖———

Alex went to spend his holiday with Nan, who was delighted to have such precious company. As planned, she stepped out with Alex, having promised to do some retail therapy.

"Is that skirt not a tad too short, my love? I could have made that from the hem of my dress."

"You're funny, Nan," Alex said and giggled. "This is usually worn with tights and boots; it's high fashion."

"Of course it is, but why would anyone want to hide their lovely legs? What about a lovely summer frock? Let's look over there at the summer range; come along!"

"Cool! What about *this* one, Nan? *And this* one … no, *this* one … maybe all *three* of them."

Very soon the saleswoman assisted in persuading the budding teenager to choose attractive yet modest and age-appropriate casual wear. She watched the bright-eyed teen mix and match items, while the doting grandmother generously paid for them using her credit card. By the time the pair left the department, they had a number of bags between them.

"Such a petite little frame," the shop assistant remarked as she waited for the youngster to choose various outfits, sandals, and sunhats. "This one certainly has fine, exquisite taste for someone that young. You must be proud. It's not every young person who would want their Nan's opinion now, would they?" The elderly woman responded with a smile.

"Nan, I like it – it's so beautiful ... but ... when will I wear it?" the youngster asked, her lips quivering with emotion.

"I said *I* would guide you, *didn't* I? Now wipe those eyes, and we'll take this *one* day at a time. Let's do some more shopping tomorrow, but we'll have to make an early start, and then you can have your hair done. What do you think?"

"Are you going to let them cut my hair short at the back and sides, Nan? It has secretly grown long. I wish I didn't have to rise early anymore to pin it up under my—"

"Nobody will put a scissors to your crowning glory. It's been hibernating long enough. Come along; you can fit all your clothes after your shower, and then I'd like to have a look at your hair."

Short at the back and sides, she thought to herself. *What utter nonsense. This child has been through enough! It might be better for Alex to learn tennis and badminton – much more suitable.*

CHAPTER 4

Alex appeared at breakfast, dressed to the nines, for yet another rehearsal of dropping the bombshell: "Good evening, Mum and Dad and everyone: As from today … *ahhh, gross!* Nan, I can't say it properly yet. I'm afraid."

"You'll be very confident, my angel," Nan reflected back. "Just remember to make eye contact with each one as you speak."

"Will do. How's my hair, Nan?" Being hard of hearing at times, Nan simply smiled and whispered a few silent prayers before they embarked on their journey.

When they arrived at Alex's home, Brigido's car was still in the driveway, and Nan was sure that their impending visit would come as a pleasant surprise. The entire family must have missed the sparkle of the youngest child over the holidays. She could barely wait to introduce them to this jaw-dropping wonder.

Alex was undoubtedly the centre of attraction, looking very beautiful in the bespoke outfit paid for by Nan. Every item of clothing was tasteful, amazingly appropriate, and clearly emphasized the inner beauty of the youngest child who had been so dutiful for the past twelve years. Alex's sisters *oohed and aahed* – in awe of their youngest sibling – especially the poise and confidence that was radiated in that dazzling smile.

———❀———

Brigido, however, stood quietly aside, as if in a state of shock. He raised his hand, and silence fell upon the room. His eyes were downcast and there were tears streaming down his cheeks when he addressed his mother and older daughters.

"Ma, is this a cruel joke? First Gerald's announcement and now this! I want *Alex* back, *now*! Why are you interfering in our household? This is not your business, Ma! Alex is my son!"

"Dad, I am not your son," Alexis intervened, touching her father's arm. "I'm a blossoming young lady, who wants to say goodbye to lawnmowers, rakes, spades, and skateboards. From *now on*, I want to *celebrate* my life as a teenage girl and *learn* from my six sisters as I grow older. And I want to be called Alexis."

"Ma," Brigido hollered, ignoring Alexis. "You have made enough trouble in this household to last my entire life. As for you," he said, glowering at Alex, "you are *Alex*, and that's it! If you insist on bringing that *blossoming lady* garbage into this house, you get *out*. I only have six daughters. Now get out of that stuff you're wearing, and man up! Do I make myself clear?"

"It's my birthday today, Dad, and I am a *girl*, your seventh daughter, *not* your son. I am tired of strapping up my breasts, hiding my hair under a baseball cap, wearing trainers, jeans, and T-shirts. I want to wear dresses and skirts, have my hair down my back, and go shopping with my sis—"

"Not in this house, not today, not ev—" His words stopped abruptly as his body folded.

"Marcia, the ambulance, quickly!" Michaela shouted. "I think your dad's having a heart attack – hurry!"

Michaela glared at Alexis. "This is all your fault," she accused. "So much for your girly stuff. Could you not be more prudent? You'd better say some prayers that Daddy does not die."

As Alexis watched her mother and sisters fussing around her father, she felt abandoned, alone, and confused. *How can this be my fault?* she wondered. *I was born a girl. Don't I have a say?*

Nan ushered the paramedics into the lounge, saying, "This is my son, Brigido Versini. There was a sort of misunderstanding, when he collapsed in the middle of it. He was always very sensitive as a child and … well … things got a bit out of hand tonight. He lost his temper."

Bending down, she addressed her son. "It's going to be fine, Brigido. Please get better. Your family needs you."

While Michaela prepared herself to accompany the paramedics, she looked very vulnerable. Nan tried to reassure her that she would see to the girls for as long as she had to be in the hospital with Brigido.

"No, Ma, leave us alone," Michaela replied icily. "You've interfered enough – aren't you satisfied yet? Marcia will see to things. Take Alex with you – Brigido will probably *deteriorate* when he sees that child again. After nearly twenty-five years of marriage in our peaceful home, you've come to wreck it. Out – *get out* – both of you!"

Alexis stared blankly during all the proceedings, barely able to recognize her parents and register her emotions. Her older sisters were momentarily lost for words as they tried to find something plausible to say to their youngest sister. Alexis just walked away wordlessly to start packing a suitcase. Besides all the boys' clothing in her closet, she barely had anything to her name, only some books from her library, music, DVDs, and a few odds and ends. She was in a daze.

"Alexis, I know you're hurting," Marcia said gently as she crouched in front of her sister, who looked vulnerable and insecure. "You've done something very daring. And even though you've been asked to leave the house, none of this is your fault. I will see you every weekend; I promise. As long as you believe in yourself, that's all that matters. I am very proud of you."

Maria stood in the doorway, touched by Alexis's gentleness, which was in sharp contrast to the Alex they had grown accustomed to over the past twelve years. Alexis was barely able to respond, and her tears remained unchecked as she listened to her eldest sister. Maria sat on the bed holding her younger sister's hand.

"Alexis, I'm so sorry things have turned out this way, but you'll always be a precious part of this family, no matter what. This is something we should have initiated as a family long ago. I know it's tough, but it won't last."

Alexis acknowledged Maria's encouragement, and when the twins entered her room bringing a few items of their own clothes to add to her suitcase, she smiled broadly. She remembered wishing for similar vests, skinny jeans, and light jumpers. Her sisters knew how to lift her spirits, she thought.

"Thanks so much," Alexis said. "I'm going to miss practising my music pieces with you and hearing all your jokes about school tomorrow. Dad just needs some time to recover, and then he'll come and fetch me."

"That's true," Maria said. "I wouldn't leave home if I were you, Alexis. Mum and Dad will forget about this in the morning. You're not supposed to live out Dad's dream about having a son. It's unfortunate that this has happened to him, but don't take any blame for this! Why don't you just keep a low profile, have your shower, and go to bed? They'll calm down."

"What about Nan?" Marcia said soothingly. "This is no way to celebrate your birthday. Go with her and enjoy the rest of your first day as a teenager. Don't let Dad's illness or Mum's collusion with Dad change what you believe is right and just. They might put you out of the house, but let your conscience remind you of the truth, which is far nobler. We're going to look out for you, and we'll make sure that you don't miss out in any way."

The six sisters embraced Nan and their youngest sister dolefully before accompanying them to the car.

Though mildly consoled by their solemn reassurance, Alexis left home with Nan on her thirteenth birthday. She smiled as she waved goodbye to her sisters and hoped that her parents would come to fetch her the following week.

CHAPTER 5

Because her nan went into depression after her son's cardiac arrest, Alexis blamed herself for her father's condition and felt anxious about what the future held for her. Consequently, she confided in Gerald Fredericks, her former cricket coach, and he agreed to assist her in finding a boarding school. She was due to start high school after the summer holidays.

On learning that Alexis would be attending Annunciata Boarding School, her sisters rallied round to organize her uniform, books, and stationery. They planned sitting with her to discuss her subject choices and extramurals, just as their parents had sat with each of them. Since neither of their parents showed any interest, the girls accompanied their youngest sister from their nan's house to the school, where they helped her to settle into her room.

Three friendly girls who would be sharing the spacious room with her welcomed Alexis. She was heartened by their warm smiles and friendliness. This seemed like the beginning of a great friendship, and Alexis appeared very much at ease with them.

Marcia and Maria agreed to stand in as Alexis's official guardians and assured the headmistress of their support and availability whenever these were required. They promised to take care of Alexis financially, attend school functions, and visit her regularly whenever she was on holiday at their nan's home.

Her twin sisters volunteered to choose items of clothing for her if she let them know if there was anything in particular that she wanted or needed. Alexis was pleased, because her sisters had great taste, and they always received the most pocket money.

Alexis was under the impression that their parents had

instructed her sisters to take care of her while their father was recuperating, and this gave her tremendous hope. She believed that her parents' decision that night had been impulsive because they were taken unawares. In her opinion, her dad dearly loved her, and she remembered how often he had told her how precious she was. Because of their solid relationship, she hoped that the dust would soon settle and matters would be straightened out. She decided to call home over the weekend to find out from her mother how her dad was doing.

Michaela sent Alexis a text message: "You chose your nan over your parents. We're choosing your father's recovery over your visits home."

Alexis withdrew into silence. She hated boys, men, her dad, her mum … and God.

CHAPTER 6

The teaching staff was enjoying their tea and sandwiches when Monique, the headmistress, entered the staffroom. She was beaming with delight as she handed over the assessment sheets ahead of their formal meeting later in the afternoon.

"Good morning, colleagues! Guess what? It looks like Alexis Versini will probably be our top student this year. Imagine, such a quiet and unassuming little miss. Here I was thinking it would be the students from High Grove," Monique disclosed. She ran her finger across the mark sheets, smiling as she read out Alexis's excellent results. "Anyway, browse through these when you've a free moment today," she said as she reached for her cup of tea.

The staff were delighted, though most of them already knew that Alexis was an outstanding student. Monique exchanged smiles with the subject teachers as each of them described how committed and focused Alexis had been from the day she started at the school. One or two expressed the hope that she would be an incentive to her roommates, who appeared laid-back and sullen. They articulated their fear that strong characters would influence Alexis and cause her to be sidetracked, as had happened with former students.

Cammy was curious about the girl's background, as she recalled that neither of Alexis's parents had responded to circulars or invitations to PTA meetings since she had started at the school. Monique had also found it odd that Alexis's sisters had signed her official school documents, even the indemnity forms. She decided to withhold this information from Cammy until she had made full inquiries.

After scanning her copy of the mark schedule, Cammy said,

"Alexis is that one-in-a-million student who makes my role as homeroom teacher such a pleasure. What a helpful young lady she is. Nothing's too much for her, whether it's shifting desks, sweeping, washing, you name it! She must have exemplary parents – such a dignified lass. Imagine their pride and joy when they hear of her success."

Monique winked across the room at Cammy, who sat in the chair opposite and nodded back. She was happy to note that Alexis's excellence was like a breath of fresh air in the eighth form class.

In the meantime, Cammy visualized telling Alexis's parents about her straight A's, impeccable conduct, and healthy interpersonal relationships. She remembered the sports coach telling her that Alexis was an all-rounder who knew virtually every ball game and that she would probably play an impressive game of cricket if she were given a chance.

The headmistress impressed upon her staff the need to be more ready and willing to study all students' marks instead of being preoccupied with star students. Her eyes crinkled at the corners as she smiled upon hearing her staff's comments about Alexis and the positive influence she had on other students, but her heart was set on helping weaker students.

Kent, the science teacher, quietly differed in his views. He was so used to dealing with weaker students who chose his subjects without having an aptitude for them. Therefore he admired the fact that Alexis handled experiments like a pro and that physics was a piece of cake for her. He dearly wished he had a few more students like her in his class and that applicants to the school would be more carefully guided in making subject choices.

Having met with Alexis's family, Cammy admired her six amazing sisters, who clearly adored her. She considered their English as impeccable and wished she had the privilege of having them as students in the school. The siblings conducted themselves well and made a huge impression on other students. She wished the school board would raise the bar and insist on stricter criteria for entrance to the school.

———————❈———————

Alexis's friends exchanged newsy conversations, and their infectious laughter was an absolute tonic for her, because she had been feeling sad and had withdrawn for days. She had many friends who showed great confidence in her, whether in drama, dancing, music, swimming, or cricket, but none of them knew how much she longed for her family and home.

"You're not interested in participating in sport, Alexis," Cass said, "but you gave those lads some solid hints in cricket, I tell you. You'd be an amazing coach, if they recruited you in the New Year. I'd be happy if you joined our hockey team."

Alexis was touched by Cass's concern. "I am interested in all sports, but I'd be more interested in those that I'm more familiar with; that is why I'm at boarding school. And to be quite honest, I miss my family very much, so I've decided to just sit and watch the rest of you. Please excuse me. I'm going to find my swimsuit and do a few laps before supper. I find it very relaxing, and it helps my concentration."

"Your parents haven't visited here yet," Bianca said. "Do they have marital issues? You are one of the best students in mathematics; you help us without much effort. I've struggled with maths already in junior school, but you make it seem so simple. I'm even beginning to enjoy it. In fact, when I see you studying, you make me want to study as well. I think you're a great friend. It's such a pleasure being in your company."

Cass signalled for them to be quiet. "Come and stand over here. The teachers are discussing you, Alexis. Don't worry; they're saying good things about you. I've heard a good bit already. I think it's our homeroom teacher who's leading the discussion about you."

The girls stood below the staffroom window and listened intently.

"No wonder Monique is so confident that she'll be our top student. She has the makings of a great teacher too. It's quite remarkable how she helps weaker students in the class."

"Hang on, mates," one of the male teachers countered. "Before you start canonizing her, allow me to inform you that she *barely* opens her mouth for prayers and does *not* attend Mass with the students on Sundays. Actually, I find that odd, *especially* with Fr Paulino as her parish priest. I mean*, no* parishioner generally escapes *his* attention. He scans that congregation like a searchlight!"

"Oh *please*," another teacher interrupted. "We've been down that road before with many of our students, but none of them came anywhere near her as far as academic performance was concerned. Teenagers tend to rebel against God at *some* stage or another. Not going to Mass does not make her a bad person. She's probably battling with something she finds hard to talk about. I was like that."

"Same here," Cammy admitted. "Let's get Sr Mary Agnes to have a word with her. The students love her to bits because of that special sweet she usually has tucked away in that 1920s handbag of hers. They get quite defensive when anyone refers to her last-century bag or court shoes."

The three friends were stunned at what they had overheard, though Alexis was pleased to note their teachers' sharp observations as well as their understanding of teenagers.

"Actually, they're quite right," she said. "Though they could have been talking about anybody. I did not hear any name, but I admire their attitude. So often children are burdened and suffering in one way or another. Teachers then punish the behaviour they see instead of listening to their side of the story."

"Yeah," Cass said. "Why don't we place our ideas into the suggestion box and propose that teachers listen to students and form good relationships with them instead of only noticing what they do wrong. They could catch us doing something right instead of harping on where we go wrong. Come along, Alexis; let's word our suggestion together. You're the writer among us."

CHAPTER 7

Although she liked helping out in the school library, Joyce thought Monique, her successor, was far too liberal with her open-door policy. Students and staff should know their place and make an appointment to see the headmistress instead of sauntering in and out when it suited them. She decided to voice her opinion to Monique in the presence of the staff.

"With all the scrutiny of examination papers, letters, and staff meetings, Monique, why are you making such a fuss about being personable? You need to be more realistic; otherwise, the students will take the upper hand, and before you know it, discipline will be something of the past. This school has always had a good reputation for decorum and discipline."

"Joyce, *dearest*," Monique replied, "there's no need to rescue any one of us and concern yourself with boundary issues. Being sensitive, prudent, personable, and softer in our approach will not *encroach* on our boundaries or time. It will *forestall* problems in the long run and, in fact, *save* time."

"Precisely," Skylar, her deputy, responded amiably. "This is something we've decided to introduce among the staff, which was suggested by our students. I think our results would improve radically if we paid more attention to our students' emotional needs. We tend to emphasize the intellect and fuss about the spiritual side; yet we ignore our students' emotional needs.

We've decided take a united stand by resolving to reach out to our students. Monique's been sending letters to parents telling them how well their children are doing – instead of waiting to discuss quarterly results. Their response to our outreach has been very positive."

"Hear, hear," the staff belted out as one, and some of them spontaneously rose in a standing ovation of rowdy applause.

Joyce smoothed her bottle-green pleated skirt over her knees and fumbled in her handbag for her earplugs. She had been using them increasingly ever since she'd returned to the school. Thankfully the atmosphere in the library was peaceful and the rule of silence well maintained.

"Michaela, what's this?" Brigido hollered as he held a letter from Annunciata Boarding School. "I thought we were going to let Gerald Fredericks attend to all communication from this confounded school. He initiated it, so now he can see it through – isn't that what we agreed?"

"Brigido, calm down. This is not going to do your heart any good," Michaela replied quietly yet firmly.

"I'm saying that Gerald made the decision and took over our role as parents, so let him remain ex-coach, parents, advocate ... the *works*. I have *six* daughters, and they are the only ones I'm interested in helping and supporting."

"Just tear up the letter, dear. I've dumped all their newsletters and a recent invitation to a prize-giving ceremony. Let's not say anything to the girls either, especially the twins – you know how emotional they are at times. They have their music exams coming up, so they'll need to be calm."

"That's right. I hope that little upstart will get the message that this family has only one head and not two. If Gerald Fredericks wants to take charge, let him, but not in *this* home. By the way, Michaela, remember – no Christmas cards to Alex, please. I *mean* it!"

"Yes, Brigido, just drink your tea and relax. Stop worrying about silly matters – let sleeping dogs lie. Let me handle the post in future. Stay away from the mailbox; you know how it affects you."

"Fine, but I still think Gerald Fredericks is trouble! I might send him an email and let him have a bit of my mind. What's he now, a remote-study coach to Alex? He's not welcome here; let him know that, please, Michaela. Sorry for putting this onto you. I knew that man was trouble when he first put his foot into this house. He no longer exists as far as I am concerned – he can coach Alex till doomsday, for all I care!"

"Brigido, calm down. I told you that I'd be seeing to the mail from now on. I'll make sure that Gerald Fredericks does not call or pay us visits. Some people don't know boundaries—"

"Exactly! You've hit the nail on the head. Gerald Fredericks has no boundaries whatsoever. Alex often coached the team without him, and he was jealous. That's why he concocted loads of excuses to kick Alex out of the team. I have a good mind to send *him* my hospital bills."

"We will ignore all mail from the school and consider the matter closed. Let's relax in front of the telly."

CHAPTER 8

Each girl's bedroom included an en suite, but the twins, Zoë and Cathy, had an additional lounge with an adjoining kitchenette and music nook. Their suite was central, with connecting doors to their sisters' rooms, the main kitchen, and the dining room. After returning from one final practice, they tiptoed into the house to surprise their parents with exciting news, but instead they recoiled as they overheard their exchange about Alexis.

Zoë and Cathy sat on their beds, their cheeks flaming with frustration as they listened to their parents talking about their younger sister. Having visited her on alternate Sundays, both girls had noticed how withdrawn Alexis had become and how much they missed having her in the home. They were saddened by their parents' cold dismissal of her and scapegoating Gerald Fredericks.

"Daddy still refers to Alexis as Alex. When will he realize that she's his daughter and not the son he wanted?" Cathy said.

"I know, but what about Mom? She colludes with Dad, instead of challenging him to see sense. Alexis is our sister and their daughter, who innocently reclaimed the identity they virtually bullied from her as a tiny baby. It's pathetic and cruel," Zoë replied sadly.

"I'm not hearing my favourite pieces," Marcia exclaimed brightly as she entered her twin sisters' bedroom. The piano, viola, and violin remained unopened while both girls sat quietly on their beds.

When neither of them responded to her, Marcia gently sat down between them and held their hands affectionately on her lap, patiently waiting for them to respond.

"I thought the big day is tomo—" Maria began as she entered, but her heart ached when she saw her younger sisters looking downcast. She guessed that they might have overheard their parents too.

"What's with the gloom, girls?" Marcia inquired. "Shall I switch on the kettle and make some hot chocolate drinks? It's the best tonic for pessimism."

"Did I hear hot chocolate?" Maria asked as she sat down at the piano and played a few notes. "I was on the phone with Alexis," she said quietly. "The dates for their prize-giving ceremony are out. I'm not going to miss it, no matter what, and neither will either of you," she volunteered boldly.

"Zoë and Cathy," Michaela called from the next room. "I thought you were supposed to be practising for the quartet in the City Hall this summer."

"No, we've another appointment," Cathy answered. "We were invited to … er …" They shook their heads anxiously and signalled to their older sisters to speak up.

"We're going out – the six of us," Maria filled in confidently, while still playing simple melodies on the piano. "We've been planning a trip together, and it will be next weekend."

"But you haven't said anything. Your dad and I wanted—" Michaela stopped abruptly when she reached the doorway and saw her daughters together. This had become a regular scene ever since Alexis had left the home. Looking very uncomfortable, she started fingering the strands of her shoulder-length hair. "You didn't say anything to me before about a trip."

"Mum, we haven't had a chance to tell you, but we're telling you *now*," Maria replied.

"Girls, we planned to have a barbecue. Your father received his annual bonus and wanted us to enjoy some family time together," she said.

"Thanks, Mum, but we've planned an outing together – *all* of us," Marcia responded as she carried a tray with mugs of hot chocolate.

"Have you spoken to your father about—"

"No, Mum, we haven't, but *you* might like to inform him," Marcia replied and joined Maria at the piano. They played the twins' favourite piece, and in no time Cathy cheered up. She was the one who was always able to bounce back quicker in times of conflict.

"This is so unlike you, girls," Michaela said. "Just when I thought we could have some quiet time together, especially now while your dad is recuperating. It would be good for him to—"

"Everything seems to revolve around what's good for Dad," Maria answered. "When last have you asked any of us what *we* would like?"

"I thought you girls liked barbecues."

"We do! But what about Alexis, Mum? What about her being stuck in a boarding school while you and Dad go on and on about her," Zoë answered, her voice rising with emotion.

"She's *upset* your father, girls; you all saw that. Be reasonable, please," Michaela said in a firm voice.

"All because she wanted to be your daughter, our sister … and … you, you … punish her," Cathy told her mother, blinking through angry tears.

"Pull yourself together, Cathy; you're nearly sixteen. Don't let your father hear—"

"No, Mum, *you* need to be reasonable! We've grown up loving each other and having fun together, but Alexis has suffered for twelve years, and yet you ask Cathy to be reasonable," Marcia shot back.

"Marcia's right," Cathy answered boldly. "You've alienated yourselves from Alexis, because she wants to be a girl and not the boy you could not have. Is her gender her fault, Mum?"

"Well … if Gerald Fredericks had not interfered, this would not have hap—"

"Gerald did the right thing, Mum," Maria interrupted. "Stop blaming him for pricking your conscience. He deserves a medal for his efforts in rescuing our sister from a false identity."

"But who asked him?"

"You've always told us to follow our conscience, haven't you? Yet now you're rejecting our sister, boycotting her school events, and ignoring her needs. She's suffering, Mum," Zoë said.

"We'll be visiting her next weekend," Marcia said. "We've been visiting her fortnightly and taking her something special every time."

Michaela looked at each of her daughters incredulously before adding, "If your father hears this—"

"Go ahead and tell him," Maria said. "Before the event next weekend, we'll be taking Alexis to have her hair done for the occasion. We have not disowned her, even if you and Dad have."

"Are you putting words into our mouths by—"

"No, we're quoting you," Maria interjected. "You've promised Dad that you would ignore letters from the school. That's discourteous, Mum. You've always expected us to respect authority, yet you callously neglect your baby girl because Gerald Fredericks stepped in to find her a school in time after you openly renounced her and sent her off with Nan."

"Meanwhile, Nan's grown quiet and barely visits," Cathy told her mother. "When she *does* visit, you and Dad barely have a kind word. Quite despicable, I think!"

Michaela appeared quite shaken as each of her daughters gave vent to her feelings. Her cheeks reddened to the roots of her hair as she held her hands over her ears, closed her eyes, and sat down. The girls rallied round, watching her closely, each of them feeling her own pain. Eventually Michaela rose and left the room.

———❋———

"Let them stand with Alex all they want," Brigido replied when Michaela had recounted their daughters' words to him. "If they want to visit, they will have to use public transport and pay their own way to and from the school. I'm the head of this home, and as long as they live under this roof, they'll obey."

"What about the twins' forthcoming music recital?" Michaela asked anxiously.

"The same will apply to them. If any one of them betrays us by going to the school, they will have no part of this home. Please make this very clear to them."

"But where will they go, Brigido? They're *girls*," Michaela countered. "Alex isn't welcome, but we can't blame our daughters; *they* haven't caused the trouble. They miss their sibling, and that's perfectly normal, but we don't need to agree with them. Punishing *them* would be unfair."

"But what if the head teacher starts asking questions?" Brigido wanted to know. "You know how Maria is; she calls a spade a spade and will easily drag our names into the mud, that girl. Remember how she answered us in front of Fr Paulino when she was only six?"

Michaela smiled. "Honey, our girls have always been loyal, especially Maria. Let's steal their hearts this summer."

"What about that Mediterranean cruise you spotted in the travel magazine? I think passengers under fourteen are disallowed. We'll invite their nan to complete our family of nine." Brigido smiled smugly.

CHAPTER 9

"Alexis! Alexis! Alexis!" was the common refrain amid resounding applause as parents, students, and friends were drawn to the petite and unassuming young girl, who politely accepted successive awards for her academic, music, and sporting achievements.

Monique Huijs, the headmistress, raised her hand for silence so she could make the long-awaited announcement. "The award for the student who went the extra mile this year ... goes to ..."

"Alexis! Alexis! Alexis!" reverberated in the room as the audience rose to their feet in triumph.

Marcia led the way to the stage with her nan and sisters in tow. Alexis radiated deep joy as they affectionately embraced, congratulated, and encouraged her while Cathy clicked away with her camera. Deep pain was triggered as Marcia recalled her parents' decision to stay home. She did her best to shrug off their nonchalance, and thankfully, the camera hid her anxious face.

"Thanks for coming," Alexis said as she whisked her sisters to their specially reserved table. "I've been anxious all week and longed to warn Mum and Dad about Miss Huijs's promise to call them. She's a very caring headmistress and wanted know why my parents don't visit or attend meetings. My homeroom and maths teachers asked whether my parents are still alive. I didn't know what to tell them—"

"Come here," Maria said, holding her youngest sister tenderly. "We know it's tough, Alexis; it's very difficult for us too, but *we're* here for you. You are not responsible for Mum and Dad's struggles. This is *their* issue, which *they* need to handle – just hang in there, baby girl."

"Let's enjoy these lovely scones with strawberry jam and

fresh cream," Marcia announced while discreetly passing platters around. "Alexis, Cathy will provide you with a copy of the DVD she has made from today's proceedings. Oh, and wait till you see what *we've* bought you."

"More presents for me!" Alexis exclaimed excitedly. "You're the best sisters in the world. One day, when I'm married, I'd like to have daughters like you – loving and caring." Gratefully she hugged each of her sisters. "Wait till I show my friends!"

As she mulled over the events of the day on the way home that evening, Marcia's voice held a thread of pain. "If only Mum would speak up!" she said. Although the girls had enjoyed the time spent with their youngest sister, they were noticeably sad about leaving Alexis behind. Each of them was deep in thought.

It's a real shame that Alexis has to be visited like an orphan, Cathy thought crossly on their way home. *Why could Mum and Dad not adopt a boy instead of punishing our sister?*

During the lengthy silence, Nan recalled Alexis's birth. *We longed for a healthy baby irrespective of its gender. I remember how I got these girls to pray. Michaela and I always hoped that Alexis would not remain a tomboy, playing all those rough games, wearing cricket togs and baseball caps. I remember the sadness in her eyes when she pleaded with me to help her. Sometimes I blame myself for the estrangement between my youngest son and my youngest granddaughter. From the time she was born, I knew I'd have to pray for Alexis, because Brigido was unwilling to accept another daughter.*

Marcia coughed to disguise the sob that escaped her throat. *Maybe it's our reluctance to speak openly and our apparent silence that gives them the impression that we accept and sympathize with them. Maria has always been left to do all the talking,* she thought.

Clearing her throat, Marcia spoke up. "Mum always reminds me about Dad's heart whenever I try to say something. I have made several efforts to talk to them in the past, but to no avail."

"That's manipulation," Nan said. "Nobody makes us sick; we do that for ourselves."

"I realize that now!" Marcia replied. "But we need to remain united in our stand for Alexis. I was so touched by her show of affection – something she could never express for years. We need to continue loving and supporting Alexis. Have you noticed that whenever she says goodbye these days, she hugs each of us very tightly. I'm so tired of disguising my pain, yet she lives with pain all the time."

Zoë was lost in her own thoughts. *I couldn't bear watching Alexis jump up and down when she first spotted us. Though it's amazing how well she's coped despite this shocking blow in her life. None of us was forced to leave home at thirteen. At times I hate Mum and Dad for causing this separation between us. They're so selfish!*

The girls remained pensive, unable to hide their emotions. Nan felt a lump in her throat as her feelings resonated with those of her granddaughters. *Will this pain ever subside*? she wondered.

"Maybe you girls need to talk to your mum and dad," she suggested. "I know this is not easy, but for the sake of your little sister, just speak your truth! I will support you, no matter what the outcome. That's a promise."

Cathy sighed, wondering what would happen to them if their father became ill again.

"Think positively," Nan added quietly. "He dotes on you more than he does your younger sister. I think he *will* come round when he realizes that you are also affected by his treatment of Alexis and the way he has roped your Mum in. Alexis and your mother used to be very close, remember?"

"Yeah, they shared a mutual affection," Cathy said, smiling as she remembered how their mother and Alexis had spent Friday evenings preparing the grocery shopping list. *We never ran out of hot chocolate and cookies when Alexis was around,* she thought. *Something that touched me most was Alexis's way of remembering our birthdays and making sure that each one's favourite snacks were there.*

"That's true. I've heard your dad saying that as well. I'm quite sure your mother also misses Alexis," Nan said. "Unfortunately, she thinks she needs to stand by your father even when he's wrong. Just imagine holding the girl responsible for her chromosomes – how absolutely ludicrous. In fact, it's quite bizarre. Whatever happens this evening, remember that Alexis was forced into a boarding school as a result of her courage. She doesn't show any signs of resentment, but I hope there's nothing brewing."

Marcia reached across and put her hand lightly over her nan's as she noticed the tears on her cheeks. She swallowed hard as she remained lost in her thoughts. *It's been a long day, and tempers fray when we're tired. Perhaps we should all sleep on this and decide on the way forward when we're rested. How I wish this were just a bad dream.*

"Shall we see you safely indoors, Nan?" Marcia asked solemnly.

"I was hoping you'd ask. I want to show you how I've refurbished my home. I can still hear Alexis saying, 'Nan, your house is like an inside-out coconut – only beautiful on the outside.'

"I tell you, I have taken her words to heart. As soon as she's ready to come on holiday, she'll have a lovely surprise. All the rooms have been redecorated. Hers is the peachy one beside mine."

The girls were delighted with the makeover that greeted them at the front door already, with portraits of each of Nan's children and grandchildren adorning the hallway. They loved the pastel shades used to brighten the house; these fitted in well with Nan's antique furniture and artwork. Yet, even in the brightness of her renovated home, the girls recognized the pain in the older woman's face as she wiped her tears with the back of her hand.

"Nan, you've always told us that everything happens for a reason," Marcia said caringly as they walked arm in arm from one room to another. "Taking a stand for our sister is a challenge we're prepared to meet. Alexis will always have our support as our sister. She doesn't need to earn it – we owe her our love and more. I'm glad she turned to you for guidance, and I love you more for being there for her."

Nan smiled proudly and warmly patted Marcia's hand. "Thanks, love," she said. "I only wish your mum and dad could have seen the pleading in Alexis's eyes the day she spoke to me about her special birthday wish as a teenager. Granddad said, 'Let sleeping dogs lie', and when your dad became ill, he blamed me. Since then he rants and raves about it whenever I visit him in the nursing home. I always warned him to stop cosseting your dad when he was a boy. Last week, Matron asked me to leave, because Granddad had become agitated. It was so embarrassing. I mean, we used to discuss matters quite easily before his series of strokes occurred. I really miss those times with him."

"Nan, it must be tough living on your own like this since Granddad's illness, but by continuing to visit him you're showing him how much you love him in spite of your differences of opinion.

Don't take it to heart, Nan. You meant it well, and as you always say, 'If it's painful, it won't last.' Alexis is strong-willed like Dad. She won't let this hinder her from attaining her goals. Neither will we."

A swell of joy rose in the elderly woman's chest when she eventually walked her granddaughters towards the car. "Thank you, my darling!" she said as she kissed Marcia and wiped the corners of her eyes with an embroidered hanky.

"Ancilla and Terése, thanks for coming home for your mid-term break," Nan said as she kissed each of them and her other granddaughters. "Alexis was delighted to see you today. Mark my words: one day that baby girl will bring this family together. I just know it. Good night, now! Safe home!"

CHAPTER 10

"**B**rigido, they're back!" Michaela called when she heard the girls' cheerful voices at the front door.

"Thank goodness they're safe. Let's tell them about the Mediterranean cruise while we're having our hot chocolate and cookies," he replied.

"Good idea. I'll give Nan a call in the morning so that she can prepare herself well in advance."

Brigido brought the brochure and tickets to show the girls and smiled excitedly as he placed them on the coffee table. *Wait till the twins discover all the celebrities that will be on board*, he mused.

"Hello, Mum, Dad!" Marcia said as she kissed her parents. "Who's going on a cruise – you and Mum?" she asked her dad when she noticed the array of brochures on the coffee table.

"We're going, as a family," Brigido replied. "Do you think we'd go without our girls?"

"Nan will be coming along too," Michaela added. "She's always dreamed of going on a sea cruise."

Maria and the other girls caught the tail end of the conversation when they entered. They overheard Marcia saying, "This cruise is a fantastic idea, but there are only nine tickets. Where's the other one?"

"Your mother and I, the six of you, and Nan," Brigido said brightly.

"Then count me out," Marcia said. "If Alexis isn't welcome, I won't go either."

"Nor me," the others said in unison, adding that they wouldn't have the heart to go on holiday while Alexis spent hers in a boarding school. They were sad at the thought that their sister was already missing the family every day and only relied on monthly visits. The girls informed their parents that they had just attended the prize-giving at the Alexis's school and how proud they were of their sister's outstanding achievements against all odds.

Hearing Marcia's opinion, Maria thought to herself, *None of us will go anywhere – anywhere – without Alexis anymore. Dad's heavy-handedness is unbearable, and this time he and Mum have gone too far. Maybe I will move out and rent an apartment closer to Alexis. She belongs to this family as much as the rest of us.*

"Has Nan influenced the six of you as well?" Michaela asked, her arms akimbo. "Why have you become so obstreperous? Your dad bought these tickets to *surprise* you. Listen, we thought about celebrating the twins' sixteenth birthday on the cruise instead of at home. Isn't that a nice idea?"

No way, Cathy thought to herself. *Why were we not included in the plans? That means that, besides our friends, our sister won't be around to celebrate our birthday. She won't be with us on the cruise, and she'll have no visit from us for over a month. I'd rather enjoy sandwiches and coffee with Alexis than a luxury cruise without her. It's no use telling them, because in the end I'll end up living with Nan like an outcast.*

There was an awkward silence in the house that night as Brigido and Michaela discussed the evening's proceedings while their daughters retired early without a mention or offer of their usual hot chocolate drink and cookies.

Bianca, Candice, and Cass decided to spend time with their best friend, Alexis, before settling down with their homework. She was such an exceptional friend; she coached them with most of their subjects as well as their respective sports codes. They delighted in sharing with her their successes, for she showed genuine interest and never failed to encourage them to continue striving to achieve their very best.

The girls observed her tearful goodbyes to her family before following her to the swimming pool – her sanctuary whenever she felt sad or missed her family. None of them had learnt to swim, but with Alexis around, they felt safe and at ease as they bobbed up and down at the shallow end of the pool.

"Dip your bodies into the water, and you'll stop freezing," Alexis said. "Want swimming lessons?"

"Not today," Bianca replied. "Let's chat. I'm dying to hear the who's who of your family."

"Oh yeah." Candice gesticulated dramatically. "Pray tell, little one; our ears are aflutter. Who are those elegant, chisel-jawed models?"

"They're my sisters," Alexis said. "Marcia's the eldest, and she's like a mother to me."

"What do you mean, 'like a mother'? Has your mum passed away, Alexis?" Cass asked.

Alexis stretched her body and floated on the water. "This is the easiest part of swimming. Come along, on your backs. Once you've mastered floating, you can do a million different things in the water."

"Nice try, Alexis, but you're not getting away. Has your mum passed away?"

"No, Cass, my mum and dad are alive and well, but I'd rather not discuss them, if you don't mind."

"OK! Then who were the dark-haired girls who came earlier to help with your hair?"

"Cathy and Zoë are my twin sisters, who are three years older than me. They're my dad's favourites, and he dotes on them."

"Parents should not have favourites," her friend said, "whether they're twins or not. Every child is special. In your case, Alexis, it's very obvious that *you* are the one who's loved and doted upon by your siblings. I'd swap my brothers *any* day for *one* of your sisters."

"Thanks, Cass, they *are* lovely. Marcia's the eldest; she buys my clothes and toiletries. Ancilla and Terése follow; they pay my fees, deposit pocket money into my account, and handle all matters that are money-related. Maria," she continued, with a pretty laugh, "is my devoted dietician, who reminds me to have proper meals, and she's the one who brings me fruit – can't tell *her* about the occasional hamburgers when jacket potatoes are on the menu. Cathy and Zoë, the twins, are very diligent, and they're sort of like mentors to me. They're outstanding achievers in music and academics."

"What do you mean 'outstanding achievers'? You're exceptional – and the smartest in the school."

"Cass is right, Alexis. Remember what you're always telling

us, 'Do your best, and God will do the rest'? Well, I've never achieved a single A, even in primary school. If you had been my maths teacher, I'd have been heading for my PhD by now." The girls giggled heartily at Bianca's corny comment.

"Bianca, you have a good brain, but you need to apply yourself daily. It's about discipline."

Alexis had touched a nerve. Bianca disclosed tearfully, "I couldn't even spell that word before I met you ..." A sob caught in her throat. "My parents ... are ... alcoholics, and ... I could never ... do any ... any home ... homework ... 'cause I've had ... had to ... clean, cook ..."

Candice moved closer to Bianca, while Cass ran to fetch tissue paper from the cloakroom.

As she rolled off strips for each of the girls, Cass disclosed, "My parents divorced when I was seven, and neither of them could decide who'd have me. They've both remarried and ... have other children now ... They ... forgot ... 'bout ... me ..." she broke off, crying quietly into the bunched-up tissues.

While taking over the role of tissue provider, Candice said in a low voice, "My parents died of HIV/AIDS, my nan has Alzheimer's disease, and my grandpa ... well, let's say he's passed on."

The girls usually looked to Alexis for strength, because she was the sensible one among them and the only one who came from a very stable family.

Her three friends were dabbing their eyes and cheeks while she listened intently and put her arms around them as best she could. They admired Alexis's confidence and reassuring words, no matter how much they complained about school or home.

Alexis's eyes shone with unshed tears. "I know it's tough and very painful, but there are no perfect families. Some parents are plain selfish; my dad is a case in point. But *we* can turn things around by being good students, aspiring towards university scholarships, and becoming financially independent women."

"That's a brilliant idea," Bianca said light-heartedly. "You're such an inspiring person, Alexis; no wonder your sisters are so devoted to you."

"Thanks, Bianca! I *have* an exceptional family, but like all families, there are flaws and strengths. But while my parents are still sorting out their issues, life must go on."

Alexis invited her friends to spend their midterm with her nan, since they would have had to stay at school otherwise.

Nan opened the door before the doorbell rang. "Come inside, girls, I've just made a batch of cookies ... I've been thinking of you." Alexis's six older sisters had beaten them to it and arrived at their nan's with the same intention.

Maria burst out boldly, "Nan, we're coming to spend our summer holiday with you. Is that OK?"

"That's fine, Maria. I believe Dr McCluskey did *not* recommend the cruise for your dad, on account of his heart. I wanted to buy over the tickets, but in the end your dad gave them to me."

"Are you sure, Nan?" the twins whooped in unison.

"Positive. Let me switch the kettle on; excuse me."

"Hello, everybody!" Alexis exclaimed excitedly. "I thought I recognized the Versini voices!"

"Alexis! Alexis! Alexis!" her sisters exclaimed altogether when she appeared with her friends.

"Your friends will be joining you on the cruise," Nan said.

Alexis hugged her Nan and sisters. "What cruise? Tell me about it!"

"You will be going on a Mediterranean cruise with your sisters and friends!" Nan replied encouragingly, and she gave each of Alexis's friends a welcome hug. "Marcia and Maria will take you all shopping tomorrow. Jeans and trainers won't work."

The girls were in shock and could only smile gratefully.

"Hot chocolate and cookies!" Alexis announced delightedly. "Very good shock absorbers."

CHAPTER 11

M arcia replayed the message in her voicemail, thinking that Alexis sounded distressed. She imagined hearing a deep sigh from her younger sister as she hung up. This, she thought, would be her chance to check on Alexis, introduce her to Dylan, and do the grocery shopping later. She swung the car around and headed towards Annunciata High School.

"Miss Huijs informed me that the school board has recommended Music Academy for my final years of high school," Alexis said. "The scholarship incorporates two years of intense practice and theory of music. I would continue with the piano, violin, and viola; participate in the orchestra; and occasionally perform before a live audience." Alexis placed the official letter on her sister's lap.

"Congratulations! We'll be invited, right?" Marcia asked lightly, and she embraced Alexis warmly.

"Marcia, do you realize I'll be moving to the Academy, and it's two extra hours by car? If Mum and Dad couldn't visit *here,* this new arrangement would be worse. And Marcia, how on earth will you explain to them your extra hours on the road?"

"I'm an adult, honey." Marcia's face softened with a smile. "Don't allow anyone to dampen your enthusiasm about this once-in-a-lifetime chance."

Alexis nodded, and a smile crossed her face for the first time since Marcia had popped in. "Thanks, Marcia; you're a gem." She watched Marcia peep out of the window and wave excitedly at someone before returning her attention to the room.

"There's someone I'd like you to meet. Let's go into the garden so Dylan can find us."

"You mean Dylan the architect?"

"My fiancé – he's on his way up to meet you."

"Oh wow!"

Dylan carried a tray bearing three steaming mugs. "Who's for coffee? I have three cups here going begging. You must be Alexis," he said, "the family genius and as beautiful as my bride-to-be."

"Glad to meet you, Dylan," Alexis said, smiling gratefully. "And you're a lifesaver! I was just about to pop in to the canteen."

Dylan grinned, plunged a hand into his rucksack, and pulled out a slightly creased paper bag. "Raspberry macaroon slices. I believe it's your favourite too, Alexis."

He blushed as Marcia reached up to give him a quick peck on the cheek. "Thanks, Dylan; you're a star. By the way, Alexis, we're planning a summer wedding. By this time next year we'll have moved to Leighton."

"That's just ten minutes from the Academy." Alexis squealed with delight. "Then I'll see you more often?"

"Most certainly. How else will I get to know you?" Dylan said. "I've heard your sisters speak of you with so much pride and joy. They enjoy quoting some of your anecdotes about boarding school, and we've enjoyed many laughs. I think your twin sisters miss hearing you practise your music pieces. They're longing to spend time with you during next holiday. Any chance of that?"

"I'd *like* that. What about fetching me one weekend, Marcia? Maybe you could tell Mum and Dad … tell them about the Academy … maybe I *could* come home for the holidays."

Her sister's heart-wrenching plea tugged at Marcia's heart. If only she could encourage Alexis to focus on her music instead of expecting her parents' change of heart – it was like expecting potassium from pears. But thankfully, Alexis had taken to Dylan. Maybe a serious talk with their parents might alter the situation.

"Imagine all those hours of undisturbed practice at the Academy. Please remember our invitations."

In an instant, Alexis's face lit up with a cheery smile. "Of course I will, but remember we charge *riff-raff* much more." She giggled heartily as Marcia feigned indignation.

Marcia sat beside Alexis, twirling her engagement ring around and around her finger as she recalled their earlier conversation. "Alexis, we'd like a spectacular wedding march, and we'd like you to play on one of your string instruments. This was a unanimous decision among the six of us *and* Dylan."

"Thanks, but only if Cathy and Zoë accompany me while the rest of us sing the 'Ave Maria.'"

"They're going to be my bridesmaids, and you—"

"Will be *hidden* somewhere at the back, *invisible* as usual, kept well out of the way ..." She attempted to walk away, but Dylan gently steered her back to her sister.

Marcia's eyes brimmed with tears, but she was determined not to cry. "I want *you* to be my little maid of honour. You will walk ahead of us and play the wedding march."

"That's going to be magnificent," Dylan said, sensing uneasiness between the two sisters.

"I don't know about that, Dylan," Alexis said briskly. "It sounds like a concert. I'd have to perform and wear a costume and stage make-up. You don't know what it feels like to be ... me! Have your wedding without me. Let me spare you further embarrass—" Alexis stopped abruptly and headed towards the door.

Marcia and Dylan followed, but it was Dylan who called after her. "Alexis, wait up!"

Alexis allowed Marcia to embrace her, before she expressed herself tearfully. "Mum and Dad will be there, but it's been two years since they've spoken to me. How can I turn up for your wedding when I'm not sure they'll acknowledge my presence? Please, Marcia, don't make me come. It's going to be embarrassing!"

Dylan crouched in front of her, saying, "We want you to be part of our entourage, and we're not inviting anyone else to play. I love your sister – your entire family – how can I not support you, Alexis?"

"It's not that simple, Dylan," Marcia said as she dabbed her eyes. "Alexis is *right*. I can understand her misgivings. We need to call a family meeting with my dad and mum, and I think it would be a good idea for you to be there too. I have made so many efforts, but they're so stubborn; it hurts."

Dylan embraced his fiancée gently. "I can't think of anything I'd like more. Why don't I come with you today, Marcia?" He winked reassuringly at Alexis, and her face split into a wide grin.

CHAPTER 12

"That's wonderful news, Alexis," Miss Huijs said, admiring her young student's assertiveness. "With your excellent achievements over the past two years, I'd be more than willing to make this exception for you. Just ask your parents to put their request in writing – we'll need it for our records."

"But, Miss Huijs, I have a wedding invitation from Marcia and Dylan. Isn't that adequate? My parents are very busy and … it's my *sister's* wedding. My mum and dad also received invitations."

"I have a responsibility towards you, Alexis. We had a student here who was injured after an alleged tennis match. News about her injuries made headlines and caused endless trauma, until the teacher recalled a letter of consent she'd submitted that turned out to be a forgery. Since then, I have been very careful – my students' safety comes first."

"Yes, ma'am," Alexis said, faking her understanding about this confounded letter of consent. Tears were threatening to flow as she walked away. Thankfully, she managed to contain her emotions and keep smiling until she was out of sight.

Feeling sad and alone, yet unwilling to explain her predicament to anyone, Alexis withdrew to the swimming pool. She swam several laps before returning to the music room, where she practised her scales and played a number of pieces on each of her instruments, including the wedding march.

She imagined hearing her name in the distance, but after looking out, she did not notice anyone. She decided to fetch her laptop and email Marcia and Dylan. She was convinced they would understand and support her request. The last thing their family needed was scandal at a wedding.

Alexis ruminated over her conversation with Miss Huijs, which seemed to intensify the reality of her family situation. She yielded to self-talk that left her feeling very vulnerable.

They're tired of accommodating me. I'm just a nuisance. Maybe Mum and Dad will decide that Cathy and Zoë should be maids of honour – they're prettier. Mum's more anxious about Dad's health than anything else, and my presence might cause another heart attack, so it's better if I stay away.

Yes, that's it – they won't want me there. They'll have their son – Dylan – the family will be complete. Dad loves him more than me, and Mum will let him accompany her for the weekly shopping. I'm an embarrassment to the family – an ugly, unwanted girl. I feel tired, so very tired; I just want to sleep and dream. I so badly want peace and quiet, rest and relief. Please help me, God!

"Alexis, thank God you're awake," Miss Huijs said soothingly. "You've been in hospital for three days, sleeping most of the time. Your friends found you after we searched all over. When your phone was on voicemail, they knew something was wrong. Was it something I said, honey?" Just then the door to the hospital ward opened.

"Good afternoon, young lady!" the nurse cooed. "You'll need some solid food now that you've regained those lovely rosy cheeks. We'll sort out your meal once Dr McCluskey has seen you."

"Doctor? Why? What's happened to me? I'm famished; it seems ages since I've eaten."

"Alexandra," the doctor interjected as he entered the room. "It's always good to hear a young lady agreeing to a meal. Nowadays, most women want to be skinny." He turned around and saw Marcia and her sisters approaching.

"Ah, look who are here. All the babies I've tended to in one family … how nice to see you … even the twins. How lovely! Are your parents also—?"

"No, they're not," Maria replied quickly without making eye contact, as she and her sisters headed straight towards Alexis.

The girls fussed over their youngest sister, propped her pillows gently, and smoothed the bedcovers. One of them pored over the hospital records above the headboard, while another opened the cupboard to pack in extra sleepwear, leaving Maria to sort out snacks and reading material. The twins quietly observed their sister while her three friends regaled her with the latest news. Alexis's face shone with excitement when she saw everyone around her.

"Alexandra needs to stay in hospital for further tests and observation. We'll discharge her as soon as we can ascertain why she had passed out." Dr McCluskey's words came as a shock to her siblings.

Marcia raised a tear-streaked face towards him. "By when will we know the test results, Doctor?"

The doctor patted Alexis's feet tenderly. "We'll leave you with your friends – looks like you have some catching up to do." He turned to the sisters. And *you*, ladies, need to tell me what you've been up to since I last saw you. Come along!" They followed him.

"See you later, poppet," Marcia announced, and she turned to walk Miss Huijs to the door. "Thanks for your call," she said to her. "I'll be in touch soon. We'll see that your three students return safely. I'll drop them at school."

Keeping up a steady stream of pleasantries, Dr McCluskey led the way into his plush, south-facing office, where what little sunlight the morning had brought spilled through the large windows in streams of liquid gold. After their very tense drive to the hospital, the siblings were now comfortably ensconced in armchairs and drinking coffee, eager to hear more about their beloved sister.

As if on cue, Dr McCluskey disclosed, "Your sister is under a lot of strain. Something seems to be bothering her. She was in a state of delirium when she arrived, calling out to your mum and dad. My guess is that she's pining … maybe boarding school is not such a good idea."

"My sentiments, exactly, Doctor. Ever since Alexis declared her intention to be a girl—" Maria began.

"Oh no, don't tell me—" Dr McCluskey looked dismayed as he stared unseeing ahead of him.

"Yes, it's been two years since Mum and Dad spoke to her," Marcia said. "They've virtually abandoned her – she hasn't been home in two years, and they won't visit her."

"It's emotional abuse, Doctor," Maria said. "They should know better than that."

"You know, ladies, when your mother was expecting Alexandra, I was so sure it was going to be a boy. All the signs were there. When it turned out to be another girl, your dad was outraged. Our age-old friendship waned, but we've remained professional." Dr McCluskey appeared uncomfortable. "It was as if *I* had orchestrated her gender – ridiculous!"

The siblings' incredulity deepened. They exchanged glances and, determined not to be detained any longer, rose and left the room, while Marcia stayed behind to speak to the doctor. She asked her sisters to wait for her before they re-entered Alexis's ward.

Maria walked ahead of her sisters, lost in thought, as she recalled Alexis's childhood years. *Dad has no idea how much we sisters suffered over the years, knowing that our sister was being reared and dressed as a boy – how Alexis had to suffer for being born a girl and the fact that he even changed her name.* Her face crumpled as she wiped her eyes. *Alexis will be fine from now on. We will always love her and be good to her. She needs our support more than she'll ever know. Nobody will stop us from reaching out to her. We'll do our best to prevent this from marring her future relationships.*

Back in the doctor's office, Marcia said, "Thanks, Doctor; we'll take it from here." She and her sisters huddled together very briefly in the corridor. Once inside the ward, Marcia invited her siblings to hold hands around Alexis's bed, but when they were about to pray the "Our Father", Alexis interjected.

"I've been managing well without my earthly father and God. Just sing something from Justin Bieber's album. It's all the same to me. God's probably on Dad's side anyway."

Maria cut in carefully, determined not to make the situation worse. "Alexis, we have free will. We cannot blame God for Mum and Dad's decisions. They are answerable for their conduct as parents. This is not your battle, angel!"

This earnest explanation gave the young girl a flash of insight into what her life would be like when, finally and wonderfully, everyone would accept that she'd grown up. She smiled and mentally changed the subject, determined to leave this aspect of her childhood behind and move on.

CHAPTER 13

Marcia and Dylan must have woven their magic in Miss Huijs's office, because when Alexis was summoned, she sensed that something exciting was imminent.

"Alexis, your sister and her fiancé brought a letter," she said, beckoning Alexis to sit down opposite her. "You *will* attend their wedding," she said and smiled. "Someone will fetch you this afternoon for your first visit at the dressmaker. Marcia asks that you wear the dress she brought recently and your matching shoes. Enjoy your mid-term break!" She reached out and shook the young girl's hand.

"Thanks ever so much, ma'am," Alexis replied. With a lilt in her step, she hurried off. Thankfully her friends wouldn't see her dressed to the nines. Maybe she'd text them later, she thought.

"Alexis!" She heard her name being called and turned around to see Dylan giving her a cheery wave as he parked his car. He got out, opened his arms, and gave her a warm embrace. "Honeybun, I'm supposed to drop your elegant self at the dressmaker's. Marcia's waiting for you."

"Oh wow!" she exclaimed as she climbed into his stunning car.

After a twenty-minute drive, they finally approached a modern-looking house in a charming setting: quiet neighbourhood, tree-lined street, colourful gardens, with very young children playing happily under the watchful eyes of their doting mothers.

Alexis's momentary flashbacks of her childhood were interrupted with cries of "Surprise!" followed by "Happy fifteenth birthday!"

Her nan and sisters had hosted her party, while her three friends, Candice, Bianca, and Cass, posed pompously in the doorway with a birthday cake – fit for a princess!

CHAPTER 14

Maria was tasked with the responsibility of briefing the family about seating arrangements for the wedding reception. Having finalized placements for guests, Maria met with Dylan's family, her siblings and, lastly, their parents. Although she expected an uphill battle with the latter, Maria reassured Marcia before her three-day spa that things would turn out fine.

Maria began, "Mum, this is Marcia's wedding, and Alexis needs to sit with the rest of us. Your pandering to Dad's moods is not helpful given the fact that we're discussing a memorable family event."

But Michaela was indignant. "Maria, show some respect for your father! He's only become sick since that horrendous experience we had when Gerald Fredericks interfered and—"

"Interfered? Oh, stop!" Maria left the room, waving her arm behind her as if pushing a door shut, and she returned to the marquee. She looked over the tables one more time, taking in the gleaming glass and silverware. "This picturesque setting in shell pink, burgundy, and cream was an excellent choice. It certainly helps lift my spirits," she said aloud.

Cathy couldn't help but overhear. *Since when do you need décor to lift your spirits?* she thought to herself.

"Mum's just queried the seating arrangement and made a fuss about Alexis sitting with us at the main table – says she should be sitting with the cousins. Can you believe it?" Maria fumed.

Ancilla squeezed her hand and advised, "Conserve your energy, love; they're not about to change."

Cathy plugged in the sound system and then groaned when she observed her twin with the video camera. She desperately tried to smooth her hair, because she knew there was no way her sister could be stopped.

Zoë giggled as she captured her sisters amidst the dazzling décor. The girls laughed when Zoë tousled her own hair, set the camera, and posed among them. Alexis was delighted to be part of the pose with her devoted sisters.

"Ladies and gentlemen," Alexis called, cupping her hand to her mouth. "The bridal couple's siblings are about to present a country and western waltz – a slower tempo to the Viennese Waltz, somewhat similar to the American-style waltz. Note the running progressive steps. The music is performed by Dan Gibbons and Pam Ford, so kindly sit back and enjoy—"

"Quiet!" their dad bellowed as he entered the marquee. "This is not your boarding school! Maria, your mother and I have a few more suggestions about the seating. Come inside, please!"

"Oh, Dad," Maria said firmly. "Must you always put a damper on things? Come along, girls, let's go and discuss this seating inside. Alexis, you too – we'll practise our dance afterwards!"

"That's enough," Brigido said. "She does not need to discuss the seating with us. That's final!"

"Dad, unless Alexis is part of the discussion, none of us will deliberate either. You don't seem to realize your need to be sensitive to our feelings, let alone hers. Respect begets respect. You're always seeing things from your point of view as if the rest of us have none. We're not *puppets*!"

Brigido raised his voice. "But since she's come home, you girls seem to have lost it … dancing in here with imaginary partners like a bunch of idiots. Can't you at least pretend to be more grown up instead of this?"

Look who's talking, Maria thought to herself. *Mum and Dad's treatment of Alexis is far from grown up. They surrendered expensive cruise tickets to Nan as an excuse to avoid her. Alexis came home for the wedding, yet neither of them have had a civil word for or about her. We've always had to speak up for our sister. If only they could see what an amazing sister she is and how much we love her. Now they want to offer suggestions, as if we intend nodding blindly in their favour. They've always encouraged us to tell the truth, but they live something completely different. I suppose I'd be blamed if Dad got ill again. I'd better just hold my tongue.*

Michaela waved her hands like someone washing large

windows. "Honey, don't exert yourself," she said to Brigido. "Here's your cup of tea and your tablet." She supported his elbow and led him indoors. "Girls, we won't be discussing anything further; your dad needs to lie down. Carry on with whatever you were doing."

The girls continued their dance routine with Alexis accompanying them on her viola and occasionally pausing to perfect their head and foot movements.

CHAPTER 15

A t breakfast on the morning of her wedding, once her father and sisters had left the table, Marcia informed Alexis, "I'll need you in my suite to help me with my outfit, poppet."

"Me?" Alexis replied incredulously. "But isn't that Mum's job? It'd be an honour, but—"

Marcia held her sister's hand affectionately, saying, "I want you to share that privilege and honour with Mum. The others had a say in the colour scheme, guest list, and décor. Mum helped me choose designs and fabrics; Dad paid for everything and drove up and down for me. But I've decided that you will assist Mum with anything personally associated with me. As soon as I'm dressed, you'll get dressed, and then Mum will help me with my veil.

"I've asked Nan to drop you at the cathedral around noon. Remember: you'll be leading the entourage."

"My pleasure, milady," she said and curtsied with a flourish, which made Marcia laugh heartily. "Isn't it strange," Alexis continued. "You and Mum used to dress me when I was little; now I end up helping Mum dress you. That's amazing!"

Marcia smiled at Alexis's touching comment. "And another surprise: *Before* that, you, Mum, and I will be having our hair done, also in my suite, while the others have theirs done at the salon. Ken and Owen will be coming around eight o'clock, and Zoë's promised to set up her DVD camera."

"You mean *the* Ken and Owen who did Maria's hair for her twenty-first birthday? Oh wow!" Alexis hugged her sister with delight. "How about a selfie with the two of them?"

"First finish your breakfast, honey," Marcia said and patted Alexis's hand. "You'll need your stamina."

Marcia and her sisters were initially concerned about their

parents' apparent nonchalance when Alexis arrived with their nan. But their sister's usual warmth and spontaneity in teaching them the new waltz, with incredible precision and patience, squashed their anxiety.

Alexis surprised them further by being at the forefront, lending a hand, teasing the caterers, cracking jokes with the florists, and even reversing their father's car into the garage when he left it outside, having fallen asleep in front of the TV. They noticed her checking things with their mum and even calling her Michaela, while the latter's responses remained curt and cold. Their darling sister conducted herself admirably, delivering her best with the chores in spite of their parents' aloofness and callous remarks. She remained composed and gracious.

Alexis waited for her cue in the bell tower, watching the extended family and guests arriving. Her nan reminded her to play the wedding song as soon as Marcia arrived at the entrance. She felt excited as she admired her satin-square organza beaded dress with its sweetheart empire waist, the elegant and luxurious V-neck, and the knee-length skirt of ruffles and beads, which had been Marcia's choice. She had chosen her own deep-pink, cream, and shell-pink wreath of roses, sola shellflowers, and seeded eucalyptus, from which her long dark hair cascaded in ringlets to her waist. The sounds of car doors closing and excited voices alerted her, and she watched excitedly from her vantage point.

Dylan and his family arrived. Their warmth and friendliness was so tangible; it seemed as though she had known them for ages. He was one of seven brothers and, amazingly, each of them would partner with her and her older sisters.

The men looked handsome in their morning suits, shell-pink bow ties, and top hats. Dylan's parents walked hand in hand into the church, waving fondly to their sons. She wondered about their ages and looked forward to having a word with them later. The youngest brother, the ring bearer, followed the last couple.

Oh wow, Alexis mused, *Dad will be in seventh heaven when he sees all these guys today. Maybe he'll overlook my gender … make a fresh start … how wonderful … we'll be a family again.*

Alexis's three older sisters looked breathtakingly beautiful as they emerged from black vintage cars. They wore shell-pink strapless gowns of Venice lace with a sweetheart neckline, dropped waist, and calf-length ruffled tulle skirts. Each of them had a side fishtail braid, set with a Swarovski crystal and mother-of-pearl hair comb.

Dylan's brothers lined up in front of the steps, and each of her sisters stood beside a brother. *Oh wow, what fine-looking couples they make,* she thought. In two ticks, Dylan was beside her in the bell tower, admiring her appearance. He spoke encouragingly to her before heading to the reserved front pew inside the cathedral, where he joined his family and guests.

Michaela and Brigido arrived shortly afterwards and entered the church before exchanging friendly banter with their daughters. Michaela's dress was a shell-pink mock wrap chiffon A-line with three-quarter-length sleeves and front and back V-necklines. The ruched natural waistband had a handcrafted flower accent and dropped to a diagonally tiered scalloped skirt. Brigido looked suave in his black morning suit and sporting a shell-pink carnation and top hat.

Alexis's heart almost burst with excitement when she saw the bridal car approaching.

Fr Paulino was standing with Brigido at the cathedral entrance when Alexis took her place in preparation for their walk down the aisle. Her twin sisters and their partners stood on either side of Marcia and held her bridal train, while the partnered siblings followed. As soon as her dad positioned himself, Alexis slowly led the entourage to the altar, smiling demurely at her family and guests on both sides of the church. She felt confident and delighted as she played "Here Comes the Bride", and everyone rose to receive the bridal couple.

"Michaela," Nan whispered, "your girls look beautiful! Isn't Alexis a picture … she plays so well."

"I think Marcia's the one who's meant to be radiant – this is *her* day," Michaela shot back icily.

Marcia arrived on her father's arm, looking amazing in her all-over Alencon lace circular-cut ball gown. It featured a bateau neckline with cap sleeves, a regal fixed double bow which wrapped around her waist, with satin buttons enclosing the lace back, and continued until the edge of the train. She wore a rhodium-plated Swarovski crystal tiara neatly arranged, setting off her up-styled hair and a veil of fine tulle with its scalloped edge.

Dylan winked at Alexis as she stood opposite him waiting

for her dad and Marcia's parting kiss. On reaching the altar, her dad was emotional and could barely lift Marcia's veil, he was so overcome with tears. Her mother came and stood beside him, and together they lifted Marcia's veil, each giving her a kiss on the cheek. At this point, Alexis accompanied the organist in playing the opening song, "A Couple of Forevers" by Chrisette Michele.

During the signing of the register, the organist signalled to Alexis for her violin solo. As this had been a request by Dylan, Alexis played instrumental music until the bridal couple returned from the registry. This was followed by her rendition of "And I", by Ciara. Her angelic voice reverberated in the cathedral amid oohs and aahs from the congregation and rousing applause at the end of it.

Alexis looked in the direction of her family and noticed that her parents appeared emotional. She longed to sit between them and hold their hands. Instead, she decided to position herself between them for the recessional song, "All for Love" by Bryan Adams, as she led the bridal party into the courtyard. When Alexis turned around, she noticed that her parents had exchanged places with Dylan's parents and were walking behind Marcia and Dylan. Her heart sank. She felt abandoned and fought back her tears, remembering again the day she had left her family home with her weeping nan.

They went to take photographs at Richmond Park, at the very spot where Dylan and Marcia had first met. Their favourite tree, with its cave-like shape, was the perfect setting for family photos. A variety of photographs were taken with the two families. Alexis was excited as Zoë took photos of the bridal couple followed by ones with both families. She planned to copy the pictures onto her laptop, starting with those taken in Marcia's suite; she was thrilled to bits.

Dylan's mother approached Zoë. "We'd like a picture with your youngest sister and Dylan's youngest brother – come along, pet," she said with a smile at Alexis. "You look divine in that beautiful dress and floral crown – like a princess! You played like a pro and sang like a bell. Your parents must be so proud of you."

Alexis was ecstatic amongst Dylan's family, and his mother's compliments were the cherry on top. But when Zoë winked at her, she knew there was something special afoot.

"Stand on your own with your violin, Alexis, and then I'd like you to stand with Dylan and his brothers," she said, grinning broadly.

"What a splendid idea," said Dylan's dad. He smiled as Alexis played a lively song instead of simply striking a pose. "Come along, boys; the next one's to be with you and this lovely young lady. I'd like this one enlarged for the hallway. Will you play another piece, my lovely?"

Dylan's mother smiled sedately. "Alexis, I don't think you've met Dylan's younger brothers yet," she said. "These are the twins, Marcellino and Mario, and those are Keanan, Lance, and Liam, and over there is my youngest, Benjamin. He will be eighteen in two months, and I'm expecting you and your family to be there. Our honeymooners should be back by then," she whispered sweetly.

"Of course we'll come," Zoë said and she winked mischievously. "We'll fetch you that weekend, Alexis!"

Having been introduced to the handsome brothers and then deciding that the youngest was the cutest, Alexis was lost in thought. Her mind was already racing around a possible gift for Benjamin. She didn't dare show her excitement, because Nan had told her it was unbecoming for a lady to pursue a gentleman. Dylan's brothers were friendly and reserved. *There is no point in being too dramatic about the invitation*, she thought.

"Ciao!" Alexis exclaimed with enthusiasm. "We'll see you at the reception this evening!" Her heart skipped a beat as she joined her sisters in the vintage car and headed home.

"What a good idea to have the reception on your premises. The marquee is such a fresh idea," Dylan's mother observed.

Michaela and Brigido smiled proudly.

"Ladies and gentlemen!" the programme organizer announced, "Please stand to receive Mr and Mrs McCann."

The guests applauded appreciatively and rose as Jared proposed the toast.

Maria invited both families to face the bridal couple while they sang "Welcome to the Family".

After the speeches, the catering company served an impressive five-course meal. Their service was flawless and the meal delectable.

At the main table, just before the bridal couple's opening dance, Brigido spoke in a low voice, saying, "Michaela, there's just one fly in the ointment," and tilted his head towards Alexis, who was seated opposite her mother.

Alexis leaned forward to say, "How unfortunate, Dad! Pity you can't fish it out yourself instead of having to tell Mum about it." Her anxiety dissipated as she positioned herself with her siblings and their partners for their dance.

She found their note the next morning.

After gently kissing her still-sleeping sisters, Alexis stepped out early, looked up through the slanting rain, and whispered tearfully, "'Honour thy father and mother' – even though they've arranged to service the family cars today when I'm meant to return to school. Is that it, God?"

CHAPTER 16

Alexis stood on the patio of her new apartment facing the River Thames and allowed the early morning breeze to massage her face with its feathery touch. The freshness of the light wind played gently with the loose strands of her hair struggling to escape the scrunchie she had drawn it into that morning.

Having spent hours preparing her music lessons for her forthcoming weeks of assessments as a student teacher, she welcomed the brief interlude of the weekend. In a few moments she would leave for her weekly Pilates session, pop in at Marks & Spencer, and then find out whether Ken and Owen could squeeze her into their schedule. She thought her hair deserved a treat after the array of easy hairstyles she had used for her hectic college days.

Since Granddad's passing, Nan had been delighted to spend time with Alexis.

"Bye, Nana!" Alexis called. She felt grateful that Nan had offered to cook her meals during the final months she had been acquiring her licentiate in music.

"What about one for the road, love?" Nan said, nodding to the bowl of fresh cherries.

What a lovely young woman Alexis has turned out, she thought as she watched her granddaughter enjoying a few cherries. *If only Brigido and Michaela would stop their nonsense and get over themselves. This child is talented, well loved among her friends, excellent at music, politeness personified, and yet, so often I've caught her looking so deeply sad ... so vulnerable.*

"Mark my words," she said out loud once Alexis was outside, "you are destined for great things, my girl. Your sorrow will turn to joy someday – perhaps not in my lifetime, God." She wept quietly. "Please, God, help her … bring her back to you … don't let her parents' rejection harden her heart from you. She's very precious … innocent … forgive them … oh, God …"

The older woman wiped the tears from her cheek as she recalled her son's sarcasm when she'd shared her plan to sell her home, move into a cottage, and invest in an apartment for Alexis. Michaela had balked at the idea and considered it too extravagant.

"Hello, honey," Ken greeted as Alexis entered the saloon. "Haven't seen you for ages. Owen!" he called, "have you seen who's here?"

"Hello, honeybun; I believe your nan called earlier," Owen said. "And how's that lovely family of yours doing? They should be so proud of you, darling. Must be eons since they've called to have their hair done. Listen," he whispered discreetly as he walked her to the door, "go home and relax. We'll come around on Sunday afternoon. What d'you think? We've lots of catching up to do. Just have some ice-cold beers – we don't charge our friends. Ciao, darling."

Alexis felt elated about having them over at her apartment. They would be her first visitors since she'd moved to Maidenhead. She envisioned the luxury of Ken and Owen as her regular stylists and smiled at the very thought of it. Her spare room would be ideal, as it led directly from her en suite. She would ensure that Nan got a treat as well – she'd been a mother to her over the past seven years.

She tried on her new outfits and selected those she would be wearing for the week. "Yes," she said and smiled, "these combinations definitely befit a music teacher. I like them, and that's all that matters."

The weather was perfect the following day, sunny and warm, with a cool breeze that made the heat bearable. Alexis felt tired. Ken and Owen were an absolute tonic, but when she recalled their questions about her family later that evening, she found it hard to fall asleep. Her mind drifted.

What family? Tears streamed down her cheeks as she recalled her last visit. *I feel dreadful about ignoring all their emails, and I've hated myself for feeling jealous whenever Mum and Dad showed them affection in my presence, especially at the wedding. I'm tired of pretending that I don't mind. I know it's not their fault, but with the grandchildren popping up, I seem part of their bad dream … a horrible mistake that needs to be tucked away. Out of sight, out of mind. My poor sisters must be heartbroken, but I haven't the emotional stamina to keep fighting, making efforts, and then being ignored by Mum and Dad. It's been a long battle. At times I hate them, but in my dreams I am always talking to them and feeling loved by them. The pain of their silence and indifference kills me. What am I to do to qualify for their acceptance? How much longer must I wait and beg?*

CHAPTER 17

Alexis drove to Annunciata High School the following morning with feelings of ambivalence: she was excited about meeting her ex-teachers yet anxious about being closer to her family home. "Stay optimistic," she said out loud, "and get out of victim mode." She accelerated with confidence.

She had prepared her piano students to accompany two who would be playing a duet on the viola and violin. The senior lecturers commented on their striking attire and excellent choice of music: "Swan Lake" by Tchaikovsky and "Jesu, Joy of Man's Desiring" by Bach. The students spontaneously stepped forward, acknowledged the affirmations, and briefly engaged in informal conversation before commencing their performance.

Miss Huijs was immensely proud of her ex-student's ability to raise the bar in the music department since she'd returned to her alma mater for her practice teaching. She was convinced that any school would hugely benefit by having Alexis as a member of staff, because of her warm and winning nature. Her ability to draw out the best from even the most recalcitrant students continued to impress the headmistress.

However, she secretly wondered about the enigmatic expression on the young woman's face – possibly a tinge of sadness – though it was hard to imagine Alexis being sad about anything. Her siblings clearly adored her. It was unfortunate that she had never met Alexis's parents, but Miss Huijs surmised that they probably compensated for their visits in a different way, either when they phoned or on family visits. They must surely have found it difficult having their beloved daughter so far from home. Saying goodbye after every visit must have been quite daunting for the poor dears, she thought as she led the students to their respective classrooms.

"Congratulations, Alexandra," Professor De Deckere announced. "You have done yourself proud. What a brilliant recital by these young performers. They're skilful, disciplined, and enormously confident. I noticed how much they enjoyed the music, and that, I believe, is the key to excellence with any skill. You're exceptional! Your assessment will include my personal letter of recommendation when you're applying for a teaching post. My colleague will co-sign."

Alexis beamed with delight at hearing her full name, and she felt a touch of relief, as this session marked the end of her examinations. She had applied to several schools; however, this reference letter would be to her advantage for each of the interviews. Her heart was set on a particular girls' high school – considered a finishing school – where ladies were encouraged to learn music as an art rather than as a subject associated with inspections, examinations, and tension. She favoured this model and set her hopes on gaining entry there.

"Thank you for your kindness," Alexis said, giving each of her lecturers a firm handshake. "I admire your fresh approach to music, teaching, and assessments. You're extremely personable; it's a trend I'd like to emulate in my career as a music specialist."

———❀———

"Nan!" Alexis exclaimed animatedly over the phone. "I've been accepted at Bonne Esperance! It's that finishing school for ladies I told you about, remember?"

"Yes, I remember. Congratulations, my love. I always knew you were destined for great things. When will you start?"

"Oh, Nan, you're hastier than I am," she said excitedly. "I haven't graduated yet. The rector informed me that there would be three of us in the music department. The other two have been at the school for the past three years, and neither of them has started a choir yet."

"Alexis," she said, "slow down. Prepare yourself to learn and observe the modus operandi before implementing anything new. You're fresh out of college, so take your time. You have years ahead of you, with many opportunities waiting for you. Do the simplest things in a great way."

"I like that, Nan. It's something I've noticed at high school whenever new teachers arrived. We used to refer to them as 'new brooms' and often predicted that their enthusiasm would peter out after one term. Had there been better team spirit and healthier collaboration, they might have ignored others' perceptions and considered the common good of the school."

"That's right. And since you still have time before you start working full time, it might be good for you to develop a routine of cooking healthy meals and taking time for leisure out in the fresh air, so that you balance your busy lifestyle with self-care. Employ a housekeeper to assist with domestic chores – especially ironing, your pet hate – and occasional baking. Although it's a finishing school, you're not meant to prepare young ladies at the cost of personal well-being. Finishing you off would be pointless, don't you think?"

"That's hilarious," she said, smiling broadly. "But I know what you mean. In fact, I've already thought about that. Cass and Bianca have asked me to assist them in finding employment as domestic helps in exchange for board and lodging. Neither of them have the support of their family nor a safe place to live – apparently they're in dire straits."

"That's what friends are for. Shows how much they believe in you. We cannot grow without healthy relationships. I wish you'd bring them 'round to visit me once they're all settled in their jobs. It'd be nice to see them after all these years. I adopted them in my heart the day I met them!"

Alexis was delighted. Nan was still a great sounding board. She had made up her mind to follow through with her plans.

CHAPTER 18

"You must be the most beautiful valedictorian this uni has ever had. Turn around, and let me straighten your hood," Cass said. "Master's in music – will you have a title after this?" She gently smoothed down the hood and admired Alexis's dark hair, elegantly styled by Ken and Owen.

"Shush, Cass!" Bianca whispered. "She will soon join the graduates in the hall. Don't distract her. Poor dear – she usually looks very vulnerable on such occasions. If only I knew how to contact her family. Let's find our way inside. She probably needs to be on her own for a while. Come along."

Alexis was lost in thought. She looked divine in her scarlet-lined gown. Beneath it she wore a stunning white lace dress with a strappy pair of elegant white shoes. She had been determined not to invite any of her sisters to her graduation. They didn't have a clue of the pain she'd carried whenever they'd visited and then left as if they were satisfied with the arrangement – done and dusted. None of them ever took enough action, she reasoned, because they were comfortable with the status quo. She resolved to immerse herself in her career and knuckle down in the hope of marriage and her own family someday. Meanwhile, she would continue encouraging her students to soak up learning.

Rapturous applause followed Alexis's valedictorian speech. That she had graduated summa cum laude came as no surprise to her fellow students, lecturers, and supervisors. Her unassuming character and her outreach to scholars on the verge of leaving school prematurely made her the obvious choice as student of the year. Children from less-fortunate backgrounds knew her as the friendly lady who helped them in the public library. She inspired reading by pointing out interesting books that appealed to children. Ten students were selected to attend her graduation on the invitation of the dean of studies after he received this information from head teachers in the area.

The chancellor, after praising the student body for their commitment and dedication, commended Alexis for her consistency as a focused, inspirational, diligent, and deserving valedictorian. "Your parents must be very proud of you today," he said. "You're not just valedictorian but a role model for these young children – a beacon of hope in their lives – someone they can look up to. In all my years as chancellor to this university, I have never experienced a body of students and educators more eager to single out a student as on this occasion. You're a credit to your family, to the community, and to this university. We applaud your commitment. Congratulations!"

Alexis was humbled by these kind words and smiled demurely. With a lump in her throat, her words barely above a whisper, she responded with a firm handshake.

"Dante, Judith, I'm counting on you to show Alexis around." The rector's voice over the intercom was firm yet friendly.

"As I mentioned before, Alexis Versini is fresh out of training and needs our support and reassurance. Dante, you'll be mentoring her, but keep an open mind. She has a good head on her shoulders; she might have lots to teach us. The entire staff is looking forward to meeting her at recess. I'll have a word with her as soon as she arrives; then I'll buzz your department when we're done and leave her in your capable hands. I'm sure greater things will happen in the music department with another competent pair of hands on deck."

"Thank you. You can count on us, Jared," Dante said. "After our orientation and planning, we'll be more than ready and back on track."

"Splendid, Dante. Judith, have a nice day!"

Heads turned in undisguised curiosity when the petite young woman entered the main building wearing a burgundy leather-trimmed dress. The staffroom was abuzz with friendly chatter about this striking beauty with her demure smile.

"Excuse me, miss, our offices are on the other side – this is for senior teachers. Your place in the staffroom for meetings or morning briefing will always be beside me. And, by the way, the grand piano in the hall is off limits. You will use the piano in Room 14 – never the grand piano. Clear?"

Then, "Welcome, Alexis," Dante said after taking a deep breath and smiling reassuringly. "Tea, coffee?"

Head swimming, she sat down on the nearest chair. "Coffee," she said with a smile and watched as Dante expertly prepared two mugs.

Judith seethed her welcome to Alexis and poured herself a glass of water. "Dante, have you heard we'll be having only twelve students this semester? Seems like we'll be crowded—"

"Jared's aware, but he's of the opinion that numbers will pick up. What's more, with Alexis around, we're much better equipped to deal with any form of eventuality."

"And I'm a realist who learns from history."

Alexis sipped her coffee appreciatively and gave Dante a complimentary nod. Dante threw her a knowing look, raked his fingers through his dark hair, and smiled warmly.

CHAPTER 19

Alexis found it difficult to breathe. Dante was a great mentor – charming, funny, and inspiring – but the last thing she needed right now was a boyfriend. Although she felt comfortable with his friendly manner and was captivated by his darkly sparkling eyes, allowing a colleague to drive her home was not something she had envisioned as part of her immediate plans.

"No, thank you, Dante. I'll be fine, really. My car's in for a service, and I've a day rider. You know how much I enjoy using public transport, don't you?"

"Of course, but listen; we've been a great team, and this calls for a celebration. How about coffee to mark the end of a fulfilling year? Jared's affectionately referred to the music department as his escape route. Admin dubbed it their daily tonic – they've even lost their frostiness – and I'm thrilled to bits that you've blown life into the embers of our music. Imagine, from twelve students to one hundred and counting. I think it's great for Bonne Esperance, and I'm convinced you're the catalyst. If that's not enough to celebrate, what is?"

"New brooms sweep clean, Dante. Besides, I've planned to take my housemates for some retail therapy," Alexis said. "They've been absolute gems whenever I've needed a shoulder during my Judith-infused encounters, inspections, and subsequent late nights. They've earned themselves a treat. Besides, I'm rather tired. How about a rain check?"

"Fair enough. I usually keep a diary, so I'll hold you to it. Come September, and you'll be as fresh as a daisy. Cheerio! Enjoy your holiday, and go gentle with yourself. See you later!"

Dante waved a cheerful goodbye as Alexis made her way to the

Underground. When she recalled the feeling of his handshake in hers, it made her tingle. *What's wrong with you?* she reproached herself. Being close to Dante – or anyone else – and dating were not on her agenda. Her summer holiday had just begun, and she wanted to spend time with her friends Cass and Bianca.

Why does Dante continue to invade my thoughts? Alexis wondered. *He's sincere, gentle, and very respectful. It's been a joy to meet him in the music hall every morning and occasionally see him admiring my outfit or my students' performances. He's positive, warm, affirming, and makes me feel special and cared for. It's as though I've known him for years. How come?*

Her gaze went up to the sky, and she said, "I don't want a husband and children, so don't even try. I've endured quite enough. Leave me alone, and find someone else to bug. Dante is a gentleman who deserves someone who will reciprocate his love and devotion. I don't need him or you."

———— ❖ ————

"Happy holidays, Alexis!" Bianca announced enthusiastically.

"That's right," Cass said, relieving their mutual friend of her attaché and violin cases. "We've prepared a barbecue. Freshen up and ditch those designer clothes for something more comfortable."

Alexis smiled gratefully as she looked over her impeccably kept apartment. "I should be the one treating you. I can't imagine what I'd have done without your assistance with tasty meals, washing, and ironing. For now, let me run up and change. I'm famished – barbecue, here I come!"

Maybe I could call Dante, Alexis considered as she was having her shower. *Surely an occasional text message is not like dating or having a boyfriend. But what's wrong with me? Why should I feel guilty for having him occupy my thoughts? I could have accepted a drive home … it would have been grand having him at our barbecue … but socializing with a colleague … it seems so desperate.*

But that's Maria's opinion, not mine. Yes, it's time I made decisions based on what I want and need. I'll give him a call later … I must remember not to sound too needy. Yeah, it's going to be a long holiday, and I cannot imagine going through the next few weeks without him around. We've become great friends, I must admit, and he's shared lots about his family. Such a dear brother he is – the only one among several younger sisters – they obviously adore him.

"Bianca …" Cass faltered as she noticed her friend's eyes sparkling with expectation. "Is there something we should know? You have that mysterious look again – the third time this week. Don't bottle things up, honey. We've promised to be there for each other, remember?"

"I certainly remember – what's going on?" Alexis appeared in the doorway, dazzling in a black-and-white striped halter-neck dress and pumps as she entered the conservatory. "Holidays are here – oh bliss!"

"Doesn't she look gorgeous?" Cass whispered.

"Always does," Bianca said and remained standing. "Alexis and Cass, while you're settling down with your lap trays, I've important news that's going to alter our lives."

"Oooh!" Cass and Alexis said in unison.

"Two months ago, I received an email from Lady Tamar Da'Versini," Bianca said. "She's my mother's estranged sister – my aunt – asking me to meet her at Trafalgar Square."

"But if she's your mother's estranged sister, you'd be even stranger to her, isn't that so?" Cass said.

"And besides," Alexis said. "Why Trafalgar Square? Isn't our home good enough?"

Bianca looked across the Thames, admiring the water shimmering in the distance. She'd been in shock over the past few weeks as she waited on official documentation. She hoped her friends would accept her proposal without unnecessary commotion, and she decided to drop the bombshell.

"I've inherited a windfall," she announced.

"A windfall?" Alexis spluttered. "Oh wow! You mean you've unearthed a family treasure?"

"My aunt's chosen me as one of three beneficiaries. She and her husband are still alive, but they've expressed the wish to support me financially."

"How touching," Cass said. "It's good you're benefiting while they're still alive."

Bianca nodded. "Aunt Tamar and Uncle Victor are titled relatives of mine who recently decided to relinquish some of their assets. They have no children, but Uncle Victor is in the early stages of Parkinson's disease, and Aunt Tamar wants to take care of him in a private facility. They've chosen me as one of the recipients of their fixed assets. The Consani Village Hotel, with an adjoining apartment block and "the Manor" have yet to be transferred to my name. According to Uncle Victor, the trustees and advisory board will continue serving until my twenty-fifth birthday, at which time they will step back, whilst retaining their titles as Lord Victor and Lady Tamar. I believe their titles are not used within the family circle."

Alexis hugged her friend warmly. "Congratulations, Bianca! You deserve this, honey. Does that mean you'll be moving out soon?" She offered tearfully, "We could help you pack, move, and settle into your new quarters – right, Cass? Though I'm really going to miss you," she wailed.

"Not so fast," Bianca said with a smile. "I've decided that I will eventually replace the Consani Village Hotel with The Three Sisters, because I'd like the three of us to share proprietorship. Unless you throw me out, Alexis, I'm quite willing to continue living here. Alternatively, we could sell this property and occupy the Manor.

"The Manor? But, Bianca," Cass said. She was in shock and tears seemed to splash from her eyes. "Both of you will have an income. I don't have much to contrib—"

"Nonsense!" Bianca said. "I'm not accepting this windfall without both of you at my side. Both of you gave me the experience of family life from the time we were teenagers. That's a bigger investment and one that I will always treasure. Your very presence contributes more than you'll ever know. So would you like to stay here or move to the Manor? Take your pick!"

Alexis and Cass shouted, "the Manor!" followed by a ripple of appreciative laughter.

"Great! I'm so happy we'll all be together," Bianca said. "Now, let's enjoy our barbecue – we'll need our energy for packing up. By the way, Aunt Tamar would like to meet with us to discuss plans with the board. I've suggested Monday, Alexis, so that with this sorted, you'll still have time to enjoy a holiday afterwards."

CHAPTER 20

L ady Tamar's voice had a warm lilt to it. Her gentle presence permeated the room as she spoke while casting her eyes on each member.

"Ladies, each of your offices is on the west wing of the building – Gregory has arranged plaques for your doors – where you will conduct meetings with staff associated with your department. Bianca will shadow Jared with finances, Alexis with Ethan for personnel, appointment, and development, and Cass with Gemma for domestics. Within two years you should be ready to take full responsibility for your portfolios and delegate supervisory members while you're engaged elsewhere. Financial benefits are assured. I will be around to oversee the paperwork until you are au fait with the business.

"Alexis, I believe you're the mistress of music at a classy finishing school. Carry on, by all means. You might organize shows for New Years', Valentine's Day, birthdays – you name it. It should be an excellent draw card – see what happens. Everyone loves good music.

"Bianca, the hotel will adopt the name you've suggested as soon as the paperwork has been dispatched, by which time Victor and I will adopt an auxiliary status. Cass, your expertise will be relied upon for menu planning, floral arrangements, décor, and various events. I believe you have a natural flair."

Lady Tamar, together with the board of trustees, exchanged pleasantries with the up-and-coming directorate, naming Bianca as chief director. She promised to visit frequently to keep the young women informed of the latest developments.

"Whew!" Bianca sighed as soon as everyone had left. "Wasn't that a mouthful? Or should I say, an earful? Two years of training on the job – goodbye weekends, hello filing cabinets, telephone calls, and meetings. Thankfully, we'll be able to sound off at home."

"Thanks for your trust in me," Cass said. "I've no idea what it's like to work in an office, be in charge of others, and earn a salary for sharing my knowledge of housekeeping. It always came very naturally, but I never thought I'd end up in such a posh environment while I'm still in my twenties."

"I'm thrilled too," Alexis said. "This is a turning point in my life. I won't need to sell the apartment, but I intend to rent it and use the proceeds to sponsor girls talented in music who are in need of school fees and tertiary studies."

Thank goodness, Alexis thought, *all ties with family will be severed at last. Nan won't have to pay for any extras or contact me at all anymore. I will not leave a forwarding address, and I'll make sure that my new number is not passed on. That way, no one will visit me and pretend to care. Let them play happy families with their husbands and children. There's no need to waste time travelling and supplying my material needs anymore. I'm an adult, and I'll take it from here.*

---※---

"I'm pleased we're set for another sunny day," Bianca said, peering out of the window. "Looks like the loading van has arrived. Amanda assured me that she would organize for our clothes to be steamed and arranged in our walk-in wardrobes – colour coded, if you please! The staff will arrange our entire apartment, so we won't have to be lifting or unpacking heavy boxes. Seems like a dream. By noon tomorrow, everything will have been settled. Dinner will always be served at two p.m. Sounds exciting, like we're in the movies."

"Alexis is on the phone," Cass said. "She seems engrossed in conversation with someone interested in leasing the apartment – a colleague of hers, I suppose," Cass added. "Maybe it's the one who offered to drive her home. Would be nice if she knew the lessee."

Moments later, Alexis entered and sank into an armchair, smiling absent-mindedly while Cass gave the apartment a final dusting.

"Needing a coffee fix, Alexis?" Cass said. "How about our last one here?"

Alexis answered dreamily, "I've just had a call from Dante – a colleague of mine. He's interested in renting the apartment. He will be here shortly. Why don't we have coffee when he comes?"

"Oooh!" Bianca exclaimed, flicking an imaginary strand from her face. "This is not just any colleague, is it? For you to have coffee with a guy other than Ken and Owen is a rare treat. He must be a very special guy! Of course we'll have coffee with Dante. Why not?"

"Why not, indeed!" Cass teased. "Is this *the* Dante, the one who likes you in peachy colours with your hair down? I'd put on that peach top if I were you, love!"

Alexis blushed to the roots of her hair and smiled broadly, "Oh, stop! We're co-workers in the music department. We're a team of three; you've yet to meet Judith."

Bianca flashed a mischievous smile. "You mean there's a third wheel? I'm sure he fancies you more. Seriously, Alexis, I'd be very glad if it's someone you knew who'd also take care of this place."

Alexis smiled shyly. "Thanks, Bianca. Yes, he is interested in the apartment; he said he's been scanning the papers for months. I really want someone reliable, because the apartment is virtually new, and one never knows what the future holds for—" She cocked her head. "I hear a car door; that must be him," she said with bated breath.

She was spot on. Dante appeared in the doorway, smiling broadly with dark eyes sparkling. He looked dapper in blue jeans and a white T-shirt as he presented Alexis with a huge bouquet of red roses and spontaneously introduced himself to Cass and Bianca.

"Hope I'm still in time to view the apartment," he said. "I had an errand to run on the way."

Bianca and Cass winked an eye at each other and began humming their favourite love song, feigning innocence. Alexis tried to ignore them, being used to their teasing. She focused on her conversation with Dante concerning the legal aspects of the lease.

"How about inviting Dante for dinner?" Bianca offered, grinning mischievously at Cass.

"That's a great idea," Cass said conspiratorially, nudging Alexis gently. "There should be enough food to feed an army. We've been invited, and there's no harm in you inviting Dante. Alexis, why don't the two of you follow in Dante's car– he probably wouldn't know directions anyway – you might continue your discussion, and he might have further questions about the apartment … kill two birds … sort of …"

Meanwhile, Dante sauntered from room to room, wordlessly exploring details and pencilling in his notebook.

"Nice try," Alexis said when she returned to her friends. "I still need to sort out space for my music instruments – I haven't seen the Manor, remember? You explored the place while I was up to my eyelashes with Ethan, figuring out dates for staff interviews and fundraisers. By the way, stop making arrangements on my behalf. I have enough on my plate."

"Oh really?" Bianca said. "The guy's smitten, Alexis. Who brings roses to a colleague?"

"Keep your voices down," Alexis said. "A woman doesn't impose herself on a man; that's most unladylike. I don't think such relationships last, anyway."

Dante was still lost in thought, occasionally stroking his chin as he explored. Then his mobile rang, and he answered.

"Ladies, I need to hurry," he said eventually. "I'm prepared to settle for the apartment if you'd give me your price. My little twin sisters are in the car—"

"By themselves, Dante? What were you thinking?" Cass said. "Let them come inside; I'll fix them some juice. They might even be hungry, poor dears."

"I could come back later—"

"But you are here now," Bianca interrupted. "You might as well finish one job. We'll see to your sisters."

"Besides," Cass added. "You might need their opinion before you make up your mind."

Dante smiled boyishly as he raised his hands in playful surrender and agreed to fetch his sisters.

"Mum phoned," Celine said, waving her mobile phone. "She'll be visiting Nanna in hospital, and she said you're to make us sandwiches for tea, didn't she Bridget?" She looked at her shyer twin for approval, and the latter responded wordlessly with a quick nod.

Alexis watched Dante as he carefully listened to the girls before checking his mobile phone.

"How about dinner at the Consani Village Hotel?" Bianca proposed. "We've an open invitation that means we're allowed to invite anyone – it's free. You're all welcome, Dante!"

The twins were ecstatic, but Dante looked embarrassed. "Girls, you're supposed to be at the dentist at noon. We've already discussed this and decided to have a meal afterwards – your routine check-up is important."

"Excuse me, Dante," Bianca whispered. "Dinner's only at two in the afternoon."

"Thank you," he said. "I'll see what happens after their visit; they might be tired. I'll be in touch," he said self-consciously. "Come along, girls!"

CHAPTER 21

"Wake up, Bianca! Are you up, Cass? I've ordered breakfast. It'll be arriving shortly – a full English breakfast with steaming coffee latte, mmm."

Bianca stretched and rubbed her eyes. "Hey, Alexis, shouldn't you still be sleeping? You need to rest, honey; it's your holiday, remember? Take advantage of the time to rest."

"A change is as good as a holiday, right? The Manor is a great place – the space, privacy, access to the swimming pool, spa, delicious meals – I *am* on holiday, but I need company."

Coming fully awake, Cass realized that she was feeling uncomfortable. Alexis didn't usually organize breakfast. Wondering whether this was a harbinger of bad news, Cass had a shower, dressed quickly, and strode towards the breakfast room.

Bianca was already seated with Alexis at the breakfast nook and in deep conversation when Cass walked in.

"Am I interrupting? I could come back later," Cass offered, pouring herself some juice. "There's still about an hour before breakfast. I'll see you later."

"No, stay," Alexis said, tears spilling from her eyes. "You're both very dear friends I couldn't possibly tell Bianca something and exclude you, Cass."

"Oh, Alexis," Cass comforted her warmly. "It's good to let it out. Take your time, honey."

"Of course you've a right to your privacy, but we've been through so much together, we're virtually family, so tell us," Bianca prompted.

Alexis nodded tearfully. "Dante is in love with me ... and he'd like ... to ... to meet my family."

"Alexis, that's wonderful news!" Cass hugged her friend

spontaneously. "What are the tears about, then? You'd make an excellent wife and mother. You're not doubting that, are you?"

"Cass is right," Bianca agreed; tears were spilling from her eyes. "You're a good person, Alexis. Taking us in when we were down and out was the best thing you could have done for us. We've lived like sisters in a regular family. You deserve a husband and your own family."

"I remember feeling loved by my family, before," Alexis said with a sigh. "But I don't feel their love anymore. I don't know how to love."

"You seem in deep pain," Bianca said. "I've sensed your hesitation in discussing your parents ever since we were teenagers. These days, you avoid calling your nan and sisters. That's worrying, I must say."

"That's true," Cass said. "But if you'd rather not talk, that's fine, as long as you know we're here for you whenever you want to talk about it."

Alexis sighed deeply and spoke slowly, tears stinging in her eyes. "There's nothing much to tell you, except that my family rejected me the day I was born. Actually, my parents rejected me."

Bianca momentarily recalled her own life history, with alcoholic parents who had left her to fend for herself and placed her in boarding school – out of sight, out of mind, she supposed. Nobody had fetched her for holidays, inquired about her progress, attended school meetings, or paid her any visits. Alexis was the first and only person who had genuinely cared and offered her friendship.

"Alexis," Bianca said. "Your sisters love you and have always visited you, taken you for drives, fetched you for parties, and attended prize-giving and concerts. How could they possibly reject you? I've witnessed their love and devotion to you. So often I've wished they were my sisters and that I would receive so much love and attention."

"Me too," Cass said. "What makes you think they've rejected you, when you're the one who's not wanting to call them? You used to speak to Marcia regularly, but these days you hardly phone her or even speak about her. You're doing the same, honey!"

"That's right, Alexis. You always appeared withdrawn, even when your sisters visited; you've never been able to justify your silence to us after they've gone. Remember how we found you in the music hall that day? But we're adults now, so you can tell us, surely," Bianca said.

"It's not an easy story to tell. It hurts so badly; it aches when I talk about it. I feel ashamed ... being a mistake ... unplanned ... not good enough ... odd ... born wrong ... born a girl ..."

"So what?" Cass asked. "You have six other sisters – how could your being born a girl be painful? You're picture-perfect stunning – good gracious me! Have you looked in the mirror lately?"

"I can understand what you're saying, Alexis," Bianca said soothingly and touched her friend's shoulder. "Your parents wanted their last child to be a boy – is that it?"

Alexis nodded briefly; then she held her face in her hands and allowed herself to cry, her body heaving with emotion. Cass and Bianca sat in silence, allowing their dear friend to release her repressed feelings of rejection, sadness, and pain.

The shrill voice over the intercom interrupted their silence, and the three friends giggled spontaneously as the resonant voice of Claire called, *"Ingliss brekfis for de laydees!"*

"Isn't she just lovely?" Alexis said. "Such a tonic when one's feeling miserable."

"You've been a tonic to me for many years now, Alexis," Bianca said encouragingly. "And I'm sure many of your students and colleagues would claim that as well."

"Same here," Cass said. "I consider you the only family I have."

"Breakfast!" Bianca reminded them gently, as the room service tray was wheeled in.

Cass, Bianca, and Alexis were walking casually up the lane towards a selection of London boutiques with elegant ladies' winter wear.

In the first boutique, Bianca addressed the saleslady. "We're not buying anything, just looking. Lovely range you have here. I love that cornflower-blue ensemble." She continued examining car coats, sweaters, scarves, and casual styles – checking price tags – as she weaved her way around the aisles.

Cass was at the far end of the store, admiring the three-piece collection. Holding a buttercup-yellow suit in front of her, she asked the saleslady for her opinion.

"That colour suits you well, my dear," the lady said. "In fact, our pastel shades this year would suit you just fine – you've a very radiant olive complexion. You'd dazzle in any of them."

Alexis was talking up a storm with three friendly salesladies, and very soon they were in stitches, laughing heartily. They appeared to be exchanging contact details, and very soon Alexis was at the door, waiting for her friends.

"Dante has invited me to see how he's transformed the apartment. Could I leave you to receive a guest who's supposed to meet me in an hour?" Alexis asked.

"Why don't you wait until the guest arrives and go afterwards?" Bianca queried. "I think it's more courteous that you receive your own guests and introduce us, don't you?"

"I made my arrangement with Dante before she asked," Alexis argued. "She'll only need a few minutes. I'd prefer it if you two received her without my being present. Could you do that for me, please?"

"OK," Bianca said. "But it won't happen again, will it, Alexis? Enjoy your afternoon with Dante, and thanks for the window shopping. I thoroughly enjoyed it."

———✦———

The message over the intercom came as a surprise: *"Specill delivery for de laydees!"*

"There must be a mistake," Cass said. "We've not ordered anything, and Alexis is out. You might like to call later." She beckoned Bianca when the doorbell rang, unwilling to answer it alone.

"Hello," Bianca said. "Is there a message with the delivery? Yes? Please bring it to the hallway, and I'll sign for it. Thank you."

Cass and Bianca carried the colourful bags into the spare suite, but on closer inspection they noticed their own names on the plastic sheaths that covered the inexplicable packages.

"What's going on?" Cass asked. "I did not order anything."

"Me neither," Bianca said. "They're probably for someone else with the same names," she said.

"Wait a minute," Cass said, opening a package carefully. "These are the very things I admired in the store; someone's arranged this, Bianca. These are for us – but who?"

In an instant, it was crystal clear. "Alexis!" they said in unison.

Excitedly, they went through the bags, examining every item. Even more special was the fact that every item had been a particular favourite to one or the other. They were thrilled when they came across a personalized card:

To my friends and family, Cass and Bianca, my token of gratitude.

Thank you for bringing normality to my life when I was most vulnerable, especially during my first year in the teaching profession.

Do you mind that I appreciate you?

Lovingly,

Alexis xx

Cass and Bianca tried on their outfits and paraded around the hallways, admiring their reflections in virtually every mirror in the Manor. They were ecstatic about the new additions to their wardrobe within a couple of hours.

Alexis arrived half an hour later while Bianca was putting the finishing touches to their evening snack. As they sat down to eat, Cass popped champagne and proposed a toast.

"To a friend in a million. Cheers!" Cass exclaimed and proceeded to thank Alexis for her magnanimous gift.

"Hear, hear!" Bianca responded. "And so say both of us to our very best friend. Our friendship is a gift above and beyond anything material. We love and cherish you as an exemplar, in spite of deep personal struggle beyond your control. Thank you, Alexis!"

Smiling, Alexis responded, "You're both very deserving and precious. I appreciate you too."

Conversation flowed easily as they speculated on what the rest of the holidays held in store.

CHAPTER 22

Alexis was clearly glowing since she and Dante had started spending more and more time together. She smiled more easily, woke up singing most mornings, enjoyed her meals, paid extra attention to her appearance, and had a much more positive attitude to life.

She and Dante took turns in using their cars for work and occasionally used public transport, particularly in warmer weather.

School concerts were on the increase, which brought in revenue and raised the bar in the music department. Additional music students regularly enrolled to their department – causing academic staff to feel insecure about their future in the school – and eventually three-quarters of the school was studying music and playing two or more instruments. Many staff members showed interest, and eventually they joined the faculty.

Consequently, Dante and Alexis considered turning the school into a music academy. Although the school board and parent body accepted and supported the couple's decision, they expressed their disappointment about the turmoil and pressure on the couple due to a lack of music appreciation by the academic staff and students.

Chaos ensued for months, until the community unanimously decided to petition the Department for Education to accommodate the free choice of parents and students to choose either academic or music specialization. The Ministry of Education acceded to their request, making it clear that they would split their original funding between the two schools until they had acquired additional financial support.

Eventually, steps were taken for the new plan, and consequently the new school was named the Alexis College of Music. Dante was appointed as the interim headmaster, with the proviso that assessments and school inspections be held under the auspices of Bonne Esperance, pending evaluation after a probationary period.

Judith planned to transfer to the Alexis College of Music, together with a number of staff members from Bonne Esperance. Alexis was delighted, because she knew that the students would be in good hands. Judith was not her friend, but the woman was diligent and loyal.

Dante invited Alexis to celebrate her victory at the Coffee Corner. "Alexis," he said, "within weeks of being in the school, you dreamed of a new music department, and Judith baulked at the idea. I wish I knew what it was that drew her to you eventually – she's transformed to butterfly status."

Their relationship grew from strength to strength as they discovered over time each other's giftedness and worth.

On a striking autumn day, two years into their relationship, Dante proposed. He introduced Alexis to his parents, Janet and Vince, who were delighted to meet their future daughter-in-law – the woman after whom his school had been named – and proudly introduced her to their four younger daughters.

"Then we'll have a big wedding cake, right, Mum?" Celine asked excitedly.

"Will there be loadth of people?" Bridget asked, nervously self-conscious of her lisp. "And will they take phototh of uth too?"

Janet stood between her daughters and affectionately placed her arms around them. "Let's wait and see, shall we?" she said.

Alexis returned to the Manor sporting a megawatt smile.

"Looks like congratulations are in order, then," Bianca announced and made a beeline for Alexis to inspect her left hand. She beamed excitedly and embraced her friend.

"You don't miss a thing, do you?" Alexis teased gently.

"What, what, what?" Cass asked searching for answers in both faces.

"I'm engaged," Alexis said, holding out her left hand for Cass's scrutiny.

"Wonderful!" Cass exclaimed and embraced Alexis. "What a rock! It must have cost a fortune. It suits you very well!"

Bianca smiled warmly through her tears. "What a beautiful ring; he certainly has fine taste – tangible proof of how much he loves you. Congratulations! You deserve a happy family life."

"Thank you!" Alexis said. She was touched by Bianca's encouragement. "Dante introduced me to his family today – such loving parents and siblings. It felt as though I'd known them for years. He has two teenage sisters, and the twins we've met have just turned six. They're a very close-knit family, and the girls clearly adore their big brother."

"By the time I was six, I was already longing for normalcy in family life," Cass said.

"Same here," Bianca said. "Thankfully, I had the two of you for the last ten years. I've savoured every moment. Although I'll miss our times together, Alexis, you deserve contentment and peace of mind as a wife and mother."

"It's all so surreal, as though we've only just met," Alexis said. "I'll be counting on both of you to assist me with wedding plans—"

"That goes without saying," Bianca said. "We wouldn't have it any other way. When's the date? We'll need to agree on specifics, like a guest list for invitations, bridal-gown selections, florists – to name but a few. We'll need at least four to six months for preparation."

"What about your family, Alexis?" Cass asked. "Should we send them invitations?"

The telephone interrupted their conversation, and Cass rose to answer it.

"Good afternoon, Lady Tamar. What a surprise!" Cass said. "We were just congratulating Alexis ... she's become engaged ... that's right, the one you met. No, but Bianca and I will definitely head the wedding plans while her ladyship gets on with finer details. Visit? Don't even ask. Of course you're welcome; come right up! You're always a breath of fresh air, dear."

Bianca felt elated at the idea of her beloved aunt coming to visit her.

"Welcome, Aunt Tamar," she greeted her when she arrived. "It's lovely that you came." She hugged her aunt warmly and led her into their cosy lounge.

"What a pleasant surprise!" Alexis said, and she also embraced Lady Tamar warmly. "It's lovely having you around – you're always so motherly and caring ..." Alexis swallowed, resting her head on Lady Tamar's shoulder and fighting her tears.

"Ahhh!" Lady Tamar cooed as she gently patted the young woman's back in a warm embrace. "What's happening, angel? I've heard you're engaged. You're not nervous, are you? Come, let's sit in the lounge, and then we can talk."

"I used to hug my parents and sisters quite spontaneously ... but it's been ... nearly ten years ..." She gave a deep sigh. "They've disowned me, and I ... I cannot ... find it in my heart ... to ... forgive them. My sisters were always warm, but ... they have never taken a stand for me."

"Alexis," Lady Tamar said quietly, "forgiveness is not about them; it's all about you. Set yourself free, and let go of your baggage, lest you take your family's struggle into your marriage. You're going to have children, and you might end up projecting your feelings onto them. Children grow up and recycle their pain in their day-to-day living as adults."

"But Lady Tamar," Alexis said, "I stand accused of asserting myself cheekily. Who will get through to my parents when I can't?"

Bianca served tea and scones topped with raspberry jam and fresh cream. "That looks lovely, honey," her aunt acknowledged. Then she returned her attention to Alexis.

"The trouble is that you're taking your parents' limitations to heart. You'll need to stop absorbing their emotions! Move on, and free yourself of their baggage, no matter how old it is. I've had to hand my assets over because my family would either squander them or scorn me for offering them financial support. Don't go down that road of ignoring your family – be an agent of change!"

"That's right," Bianca said. "You only weaken your stand when you practise tit for tat. Yes, they've rejected you, but don't reject them back. You'll find yourself doing exactly the same. Pay them back with kindness – reclaim your power and your energy. You deserve better!"

"So what must I do, Bianca? Go back and wear male clothes, clean the yard, and paint the conservatory?"

"Of course not," Bianca said encouragingly. "Why don't we visit them and hand-deliver your invitations? We might be pleasantly surprised."

"No, be a little more sensitive," Lady Tamar said gently. "Your parents know deep down where the fault lies. Allow them the space they need. Time might be a great healer, but it's what we do with the time that matters. Be creative. Send them invitations as you'd do for all your guests. Remain polite and respectful; that's more adult. I wouldn't expose them!"

"Have a scone," Cass said as she settled the tray she had so lovingly prepared. "It's good for heartache."

CHAPTER 23

The next couple of months flew by. Dante and Alexis arranged to meet one more time with the director of property development to discuss their housing prospects. They had previously agreed to discuss the terms and conditions privately before returning with their decision and signing any documents. The idea of living in a complex was not something Alexis had envisaged as ideal, but when the director explained the safety and security measures for residents, she understood. They looked forward to their two-week holiday before the final term.

"We could be ready with your house within eight to ten months, weather permitting – you're free, of course, to come over at any time to check on its progress – by which time you will have had time to acquire any additional furniture, curtaining, and other household items."

"That's going to be rather challenging for us. I love carpets and pastels, but Alexis likes knotty pine, earthy and natural tones, and laminated flooring," Dante disclosed while glancing caringly at his fiancée.

The director handed them a portfolio of various floor designs and colours. "Glad you've said that. We provide the flooring and built-in cupboards in the kitchen, laundry, bedrooms, and garage areas, according to the couple's taste, as long as it is within our range.

"Have a look at our carpet collection and tiling for certain areas and the natural look in others. I'll leave you to discuss your preferences. Simply quote the codes in your floor plan, and let me have them within a week at latest."

Dante and Alexis left the director's office smiling broadly. They were glad to have had a chance to express their needs for their own personal touches in their new home.

Alexis recalled how decisions had been taken in her home and how she had been expected to conform.

Mum gave each of my sisters a mirror in her room, and I had to make do with one inside my wardrobe. I wasn't allowed a carpet, because she and Dad suspected that I'd leave it grubby with mud from my cricket togs. I had no say about my bedroom colour scheme – my curtains were boyish and busy. I had to accept their choices. Even my chores were masculine; no wonder Coach was concerned about me lifting heavy things. Mum took offence when I told her this.

Dante's light touch on her shoulders instantly lifted Alexis from the past, and she smiled as he gallantly opened the car door for her.

"Lady Tamar has kindly offered us the Manor until our house is completed!" Alexis announced as they drove away. "She's suggested that we use the master bedroom – of course, only when we're married. What do you think?"

"She's mentioned it to me, as well," Dante said. "But I feel somewhat uncomfortable, Alexis. I should be the one providing a temporary home." He parked outside their favourite Coffee Corner and winked at her.

Alexis chose their usual corner seats, while Dante ordered their regular filter coffee with raspberry macaroons before returning to his seat to await their tray.

"What about the apartment?" Dante inquired. "I wouldn't like to see it go to just anyone; every inch of that place is special. Any ideas?"

Then, from somewhere deep inside, a memory was awakened of something that had given her freedom once. "Your sister Verushkah goes to college next year, and I'm sure she'd be delighted to have her own apartment close by. Your mum and dad might feel sad about her moving out, but it's a cheaper option. You could pay the rent there, if that'd make you feel better about making a contribution. I'm sure your parents would welcome any financial assistance."

Dante smiled broadly. "That's brilliant! I'd love to ease their financial load – there are three more to educate. Once we're married and settled, they might continue paying Verushkah's rent and utilities. Yeah, that's a reasonable option. I'll speak to my parents this evening."

"Bridget and Celine will obviously miss you and their big

sister," Alexis said and smiled. Anoushkah told me recently that she'd be happy to have Verushkah's bigger room and en suite, because she'd use her own bedroom as her private study, if you please. She's quite grand at fourteen, I'll say. You're truly blessed with beautiful sisters, as well as very supportive parents."

Dante nodded as he sipped his coffee and smiled gently. His mind wandered way beyond the Coffee Corner.

I'd love to have sons someday; girls are quite awkward. I'd have to be smoulderingly rich to afford all the things girls want and need. At six, Celine and Bridget need so many things, besides Barbie dolls and ketchup. I'd load my luggage in a day, whereas young Anoushkah would need a week to move from one room to another. I bet she'll stuff every nook and cranny in her study with all kinds of paraphernalia. Well, I suppose she'll also need space for her musical instruments and a place to practise. Girls!

———————❖———————

"Alexis, Lady Tamar and Lord Victor are very warm and loving – one would think you're the one related to them, not Bianca. What was that tête-à-tête all about?" Dante asked.

Alexis moved forward, her slender hand tenderly brushing Dante's arm. "Lady Tamar and Lord Victor have offered to take charge of our wedding – Cass and Bianca will assist them. I've requested that if any of my family inquires, I'd like them to be guests of honour rather than the ones slaving around to assist me. They did enough when I was growing up."

"Isn't that very noble of them," Dante said. "Such caring people. I really admire them. I am concerned, though, that you want your family to attend as guests. Whatever for, Alexis?"

"Dante, have you listened to what I just said? We're from different worlds. Don't expect me to go traipsing up and down to keep up appearances. My family disowned me. I am not likely to go 'round begging for their love and attention." She rose and walked towards the car.

"But they might not see it that way," Dante said, sliding into the car beside her. "Keep an open mind. I'm sure they'd do more for you if they could. I know your dad does not seem easy to relate to. But I've made an appointment with him through the parish priest, Fr Paul—"

"You did not!" Alexis said.

"I had to. You've met my parents, and I've wanted to meet yours. I spoke to Fr Paulino, and I've asked him to arrange a meeting between my parents and yours. He promised he'd do so."

"What are you saying?" Alexis said, fanning her face with an improvised fan. "I can't believe you've done this without consulting me … going behind my back! How could you?" She whipped out her phone to call a taxi and stepped back out of his car. "I'll find my way home – no need to wait."

"Alexis, we need to be objective here," Dante pleaded, following her. "I dearly want to meet your family too. It's common courtesy for a man to make his intentions of marriage known to the woman's parents. Please, let's talk this over. Come with me. We can't part like this!"

"I have never been so humiliated, Dante! How could you have deceived me and made secret plans with the priest who has to officiate at our wedding?" Her eyes burnt with reproach.

"It was not intended to be a secret. I planned to talk to you about it when the time was right."

"Splendid! Then meet with him again – only this time, tell him the wedding is off. Goodbye!"

Words failed him when he saw her driving off in a taxicab, and his eyes were stricken with anguish.

Alexis headed for the hotel where an engagement party was to be held for her and Dante. She made a beeline for Lady Tamar's suite, hoping there'd still be time to call off the celebration.

"Good evening, Lady Tamar!" Alexis spoke under her breath when she eventually found Lady Tamar in the dining hall speaking to the caterers. "Please excuse me, but something unforeseen has come up. Please excuse me. I'll probably only see you on Monday or Tuesday."

Lady Tamar took a breath of astonishment. Could she have heard correctly? "I don't understand, Alexis. This dinner has been specially arranged for you and Dante to celebrate your engagement! We promised you a celebration. Where is he? Has there been an accident … it's not bad news, is it? His family will be coming and some of your colleagues as well. We can't call it off. Talk to me – what's going on?"

"Please, I can't explain it right now … I'm feeling unwell. I'll explain another time. Make some excuse ... say something ... anything." She mumbled her gratitude and then turned to leave, looking dazed and feeling vulnerable.

Lady Tamar opened her mouth to protest, but before she knew it, Alexis had left. Something seemed terribly wrong. She decided to tell the guests they were celebrating the renaming of the hotel instead. Fortunately, the invitations had been done telephonically and no mention made of the engagement. Lady Tamar had grown very fond of Alexis and was determined to pull out all the stops to make her wedding a memorable event.

Alexis returned to the Manor feeling emotionally drained and very exhausted. She curled up under her duvet, fully clothed, and heard a piercing noise that seemed to come from far away. Then it dawned on her that it was coming from deep inside her. It was an intense moan of grief and despair, which felt like the floodgates of her grief had been torn open. She sobbed uncontrollably for what seemed like hours, hugging a pillow to muffle the sound.

Her mind switched to the endless thoughts she'd had in the taxicab on her way home:

Happiness and peace constantly seem to elude me. The worst-case scenario usually happens in my life over and over again. It's as if I have to continue being a doormat for peace to prevail. Mum and Dad always made decisions about me. While my sisters could argue or sulk, I was expected to man up, grin, and bear it. I feel worthless and unimportant. Does anyone love me? Am I fit to be married? Am I God's mistake? I'll probably end up as a boring spinster who stays home and lets life pass her by. In any case, I'm not pretty. Dante likes music, and now that he's the head, I'll fade out of his life. I hope he'll find a more acceptable and normal woman.

It was in the early hours of the following morning that Bianca found Alexis – still in her day clothes – fast asleep in the spare bedroom.

She tiptoed out and returned to the phone. "Yes, Aunt Tamar, she is here. That sounds reasonable. Cass and I will be out anyway. Ta-ra!"

CHAPTER 24

D ante's mother, Janet, came into the kitchen and found her son sitting with his favourite mug, but she noticed that the kettle did not contain enough water even for a single cup.

"You and Alexis missed an exciting celebration last night. I thought you'd be there. Lord and Lady Versini officially handed over their assets to 'The Three Sisters' – whoever they are. She did not name anyone, but she said these would be announced and published in due course."

The previous day's parting with Alexis remained a blur in Dante's mind amid all that had happened. How quickly everything had changed. Why didn't his mobile ring so he could hear Alexis's voice? He felt empty, confused, overwhelmed and desperately sad. If only his mother would leave him in peace and go back to bed. He wanted to be alone and sort things out in his mind.

Silence. Not a good sign at all, she thought. "Is anything the matter, Dante? Let me make that coffee—"

"Stop! I want to be left alone … I can make my own coffee. Just go …" He sounded utterly helpless. "This is between us. I'm an adult … can deal with my issues myself … please leave!"

Janet closed the kitchen door. Vince and the girls were fast asleep. She sensed that her son needed her. This time she would not miss the chance to find out. Wrapping her bathrobe tighter, she prepared their cups for lemon-and-ginger flavoured tea. She sat opposite him, held both his arms firmly, and looked into his eyes. There was that look again – of anguish, pain, and depression. *Not again, please, God,* she silently prayed.

"Dante! Has something happened? I'm not going anywhere until you talk. You promised you wouldn't keep secrets from me while you're under this roof. So let it out! Now!"

He spoke sadly. "I thought it was going to turn out fine ... good for both of us. I always worried about her not having her family around ... she's always doing things for others ..." He choked on his words, struggled to contain his emotions and, eventually, sobbed helplessly. "I didn't mean to go behind her back. I just ... wanted to do something good and ... give her the happiness she deserves, Mum. She deserves to be loved and nurtured ... she needs her family ..."

"Of course she does; we both know that. And you tried to help; tell me about it."

"I made an appointment to visit her parents. Isn't it chivalrous to ask for a woman's hand in marriage? I wanted to do the right thing, but seemingly it wasn't. She's so hurt, and we parted company yesterday ... I'm not sure she ever wants to see me again. It hurts so much ..."

He continued sharing his sadness while his mother listened, allowing him to let it all out. When his sobbing subsided, Janet rose and poured their tea. She rubbed his arms affectionately and spoke in a gentle voice.

"Dante, because you love Alexis, you instinctively care for her family already. I understand that. Your intentions are noble, and they come from a loving heart. Don't discount that. However much your actions have hurt her, *you* haven't. She's been hurting for a while."

"I *have* hurt her, Mom, by not including her in my decision—"

"Is that what the priest told you?" she asked gently. "Has he spoken to you about doing things behind your fiancée's back?"

"No, he hasn't. In fact, he predicted that it would be a problem, because it's been years since her father turned his back on her." His face trembled with pain as he continued. "How could a father turn his child away at thirteen years of age, Mum? She's such a dear person ..."

"Dante, remember the day Sasha returned from the vet as a young puppy? She'd received a series of injections, and you tried to touch her; do you recall what happened?"

"Yes, she snapped at me. But what has Sasha got to do with all this? She's grown big and lovable. She lets me touch her now – even looks out for touches."

"The point is that she was in very deep pain and even your kind hand near her wound was threatening. Over the years her trust grew, and she allowed you to tend to her. It did not happen overnight, did it?"

"No, not at all! I think I've acted too hastily and triggered Alexis's anger. She might have felt threatened and turned away – not necessarily from me, but from her pain – but she needs me more than ever now, Mom. I unleashed her anger, but her reaction has a deeper history."

"You must have done something particularly helpful to win Sasha over – do you remember?"

"Yeah! Lots of patience, and I've had to be very gentle – that's it, Mom!" His face lit up, and leaning across, he gave her a huge hug. "That makes so much sense. We *will* be married, Mom, and I'm going to tread very lightly and allow Alexis to manage her own struggles. My going ahead of her might have been misconstrued as being forceful, arrogant, and intimidating."

"Son, trust takes time – it's an important quality for a good marriage – and parenthood is one vocation that is not learnt like academics. Prepare yourself for deeper learning by being open to it. After God, she's to be your top priority when you're married – your queen."

She leaned over and patted her son's hand. "Go and have some rest – you've a long day ahead."

CHAPTER 25

Alexis stepped out of the shower still feeling tired, but she was determined to spend some quality time organizing her sheet music. Within a week she would be back at school practising with the choir in preparation for the music festival.

She emerged from her bedroom wearing a flowing canary-yellow dress teamed with a pair of white sandals. A smile played on her face when she noticed Lady Tamar at the lounge table reading the newspaper. She was about to offer the elderly lady something to drink when the shrill voice on the intercom invited, *"Brekfiss for de laydees!",* sending her into fits of giggles.

"Thank you," she responded warmly, for she was famished, not having eaten for a full day.

"I'd love to join you," Lady Tamar said. "Victor's spending time with my sister-in-law, and they'll probably be popping in here afterwards. She's been longing to speak to him for a while, but her husband – a bit of a hypochondriac, I think – always demands so much of her time. She's finally decided to meet with Victor, because her mother-in-law promised to be around and tend to her son's needs. Don't ever become your husband's handmaid, Alexis!"

"Shall I organize dinner for Lord Victor and the Lady?" Alexis inquired, politely ignoring her last remark.

"My dear, her husband waived his title years ago, so you will simply address her by her first name, unless she prefers her surname. We've always been very close, but over time we've lost contact. She has beautiful children, whom I met when they were very young, but with the business, we've been up to our eyelashes.

"Victor's organized the paperwork for her husband, which

she's come to settle, and we'll have dinner in the hotel afterwards. She's not expecting me at all. It's all meant to be a surprise. You're free to join us, of course."

"Thanks, I'd love that," Alexis said. "But maybe another time. I've a bit of a headache. She'll probably visit a few more times, won't she?"

"Most likely. Victor's father invested a lump sum for each of his children in a trust fund. His youngest brother chose to accumulate his and eventually share it equally among his children when their last-born got married. Victor, being the eldest, requested several times that his siblings come forward and claim their inheritance. Their younger brother had donated his share to the parish priest and asked him to use it for a worthy cause."

"I wonder if he ever regretted abdicating his rights to a title. It seems an awfully bold decision to make in this day and age," Alexis said. "I'm impressed at his generosity towards his children though. He must love them dearly."

Alexis received the breakfast tray gratefully. She arranged the plates and cutlery in the breakfast nook before inviting Lady Tamar to join her. "Please join me for breakfast, Lady Tamar. I'm starving."

"I should think so," Lady Tamar said. "You skipped your favourite dish last night – we missed you. Dante did not show up either. Don't tell me there's already trouble in paradise!"

Alexis buttered her toast. She wanted to forget the incident, but just hearing his name brought a fresh flow of tears. She tried her utmost to dismiss Lady Tamar's questioning tone, but eventually she succumbed to the deep pain in her heart and allowed her tears to flow freely.

"Oh, Lady Tamar …" she started, unable to articulate her words. Lady Tamar gently touched her wrist, allowing her to release her deep pain.

"Tension is healthy, Alexis! Victor and I married young, and even though we're well into our sixties, we still have regular fights, without loving each other less."

Alexis sat up and stared at Lady Tamar. "Is that true? I mean … that you two still fight? My mom and dad never disagreed with each other. They only disagreed with us … and I thought … I thought they were being loyal to one another."

"Loyal? My foot!" Lady Tamar said, and she smiled when she heard Alexis giggling at her remark.

"Dad would get upset," Alexis started, as fresh tears welled in her eyes. "And Mum would back him up. She did not listen to us. She covered up for him and left us feeling as if we had no right to an opinion. We had to agree with them, but they did not listen to our side – never, ever. It was so frustrating. I'm afraid, Lady Tamar, afraid that I will be a disloyal wife."

"Alexis, I'd be more afraid if you were a puppet or a spineless wannabe martyr. You're an intelligent woman with a golden career ahead of you. You're an adult, and you won't abdicate that role, will you?"

Having regained her composure, Alexis felt at ease sharing her story with Lady Tamar. Although she laughed at Lady Tamar's comments, she realized that she had never been this open with anyone before. She felt free to express herself in a safe environment, because the more she shared, the more she felt tension being released from her body.

Lady Tamar's voice was tender as she said, "You cannot fix your family, darling. You might have to do the most difficult thing of all – nothing. Time is the greatest healer."

"Thank you, Lady Tamar! Today you've made me realize how much mothering I still need. I've had to parent myself, so to speak, and adopt friends as my siblings."

"And you've done a pretty good job. Bianca and Cass have had no experience of a healthy family life either. I believe one of your mutual friends, Candice, is doing very well, and she attributes her success to your influence and encouragement."

"She's done the work herself. I learnt from her as well. As for Bianca and Cass, they have been family to me; they've met my sisters and Nan, but I've severed contact with them – it was too painful having them visit me as if I were in prison. I wanted more, not the dregs of family life."

"I can understand that. It sounds as though they've continued their lives without you, made plans around you, and excluded you. Although you've accumulated enough financially and materially, you've been starved emotionally. Yes, that sounds pretty tough."

"My mother and I were close. I miss her so much and wish she would spend time listening to me. You remind me so much of her – there's something in your tone of voice that's similar to hers. That's why I took an instant liking to you the day we met in the Consani Village Hotel."

"That must be telepathy, Alexis, because when I first met you,

I thought that you, rather than Bianca, would pass as my niece. You resemble my family far more than she does. Speaking of which, let me show you some photographs on my iPad."

"Lady Tamar, we've been nibbling at our breakfast like naughty schoolgirls. Why don't we finish, then I'll clear the trays, and we'll sit down in the lounge and look through your photos. I have my own collection, and you might want to see them as well."

"I'd love that. Alexis, you've a tremendous ability to park your emotions – a great ingredient for marriage. These ups and downs are normal in healthy relationships. What is it that you really want from your relationship with Dante?"

"I would like to get married and have a family. You've helped me clear away some of my emotional cobwebs."

"But I've not done anything except listen to you," Lady Tamar said gently over the meal. "I only wish I could make it all better, Alexis."

"You've already helped so much by listening to me. It's all I've ever needed – a listening ear."

"Dante is very blessed to have you. He comes from a good family, and from what you've told me, his experience of family life is very healthy and balanced. It's a shame things turned out for you that way, but it would do you the world of good to remember always that heartache is never the end of the journey."

"Yeah, I believe that in a way, but it's not that simple when one is in the midst of pain. I think recalling the experience of the pain and then sharing it with someone is only part of the learning. The real work involves moving on. That's where I feel a sort of stuck-ness. I need to find my way out of it – because there's a part of me that wants to hold on. I'm not sure why."

"Dante cannot be expected to mind-read your feelings. How do you see the way forward in your relationship, especially in matters about your family?"

"Maybe I could share a little more about myself. I must say I felt ashamed to tell him about them wanting a boy. I think it would help if he were patient and allowed me time to heal, because *I'm* not the one who walked out on *them*. My parents ..." Alexis fought back her tears and swallowed hard. "My parents disowned me, and you're asking me about the way forward in *my* relationship." She shook her head in despair.

"Alexis, I know that it must hurt very deeply; no wonder

you're hesitant to let Dante meet them. But, believe it or not, their pain is deeper. One day all this will be clearer to you."

Alexis was struck by Lady Tamar's wisdom and marvelled at her healthy outlook on life. Suddenly she felt a desire to blossom into her own person – resilient, resolute, and assertive – and refuse to be a victim. She was going to reclaim her inner strength and face her struggles head-on.

CHAPTER 26

Alexis had gone downstairs towards the car park and was about to enter her car when she heard Dante's voice behind her. She was excited, a little uneasy, determined, but nervous. Everything was whirling round in her mind, and butterflies fluttered in the pit of her stomach.

She knew she owed him an apology, but she was unsure whether she could seize the moment.

Dante leaned into the car and gently touched her hand on the steering wheel. "Do you believe two people can be destined to be together forever?" he asked her gently.

Alexis climbed out of the car and nervously smoothed down her dress. "I suppose so." She held his hand as he reached out for hers and looked into his eyes. A dazzling smile lit up her face, and she felt her heart taking a tumble. "I think we're well on the road to our destiny."

"I've been clumsy, Alexis. I'm so sorry! I promise to make up to you for it. Fresh start?"

"Fresh insights. There are two of us in this relationship, and I've hurt you too. Forgive me."

Alexis admired the way he tugged at his hair whenever he felt embarrassed. This time, however, his smile lit up his face, transforming it from the bookish headmaster aspect into something warm and friendly. She stole a glance at his attire and noted how smart he looked in his white wool sweater and royal-blue flannel trousers.

For a precious instant their gaze locked, until Dante broke the silence. "Don't you think it's providential that we will be staying in the Manor until our house is ready? We'll have ample time and space to give our relationship a chance before we settle into our new home."

She smiled up at him. "I could live under a bridge, as long as I could be with you forever."

He gently touched her cheek with the back of his hand. "That's my girl! Let's use my car – I've parked over there – and visit our favourite Coffee Corner."

"Why not? I'd love scones with strawberry jam and fresh cream today."

"Mmm! Sounds good to me."

As the weeks passed, Dante and Alexis settled happily into their new work routine. Highlights for the year included mid-year assessments, the annual music festival, and recruiting of new staff to the faculty. They were determined to embark on participative leadership and engage the staff members according to their strengths and expertise.

Dante and Alexis envisaged a healthy partnership between the colleges and the community and chose Judith to take responsibility for social gatherings as part of staff development. Surprisingly, she arranged a music extravaganza and invited their erstwhile colleagues, students, parents of Bonne Esperance, and the local community to attend.

The entire staff was highly impressed with Judith's initiative of a social and financial enterprise. Two of their skilled community leaders, Lizzie and Elaine, jumped at the opportunity to assist with ticket sales and advertisements. Their husbands, Jean-Pierre and Sean, promised to secure parking for patrons.

The choir practised a number of songs from their repertoire with the junior and senior orchestra, and according to the choir mistresses, Judith and Martha, both groups were improving by the day. Alexis praised them for their warm rapport with students and encouraged them to continue building up healthy interpersonal relationships among students.

Excitement was mounting among students and their parents as the date for the music extravaganza drew closer.

At the staff meeting, Dante invited an update of preparations and practicalities.

Alexis smiled. "I cannot enter the supermarket without someone telling me how much they're looking forward to the forthcoming concert. It looks like we're going to need more than one night's performance."

"I agree," Judith said. "When I was at the butcher's over the weekend, some of the customers said that although their children were not musically inclined, they felt honoured to be invited to a performance at an affordable price."

Gabriel, who had recently celebrated his fiftieth birthday, excitedly raised his hand. "Some of my ex-students have queried, 'You mean a real orchestra?', and when I shared with them about the progress we're making with our own CD, they offered to initiate scholarships for talented, but needy, students."

"That's wonderful, Gabriel!" Dante said. "Was that a suggestion or a plan they have in mind?"

"As a matter of fact, Dante, they've promised to meet with Alexis."

"Alexis?" everyone exclaimed in unison, followed by appreciative laughter and applause.

Dante winked at Alexis. "Nobody meets with Alexis without my permission!"

More laughter followed, and Alexis blushed to the roots of her hair. "Dante, I told you this morning about the letter I received from one of the town councillors and his proposal."

This time it was Dante's turn to tease Alexis. "How could I be comfortable about someone making a proposal to my fiancée? I had no idea about a scholarship ... I feel intimidated ... he's probably more handsome – but a proposal, that's outrageous!"

There was an outburst of hilarity as the staff teased Dante relentlessly, while he drummed his fingers on the desk, laughing with embarrassment. When he was able to regain his composure, he said, "I will jealously guard my fiancée if I suspect even the slightest interference."

Alexis went over and sat on his lap. "Nobody will trade places with *my* fiancé and confidante."

The staff spontaneously rose and sang with full gusto, "For they are jolly good fellows!"

CHAPTER 27

C eline and Bridget must have been the cutest six-year-olds in the world on their brother's wedding day. Fr Basil, the new parish priest, smiled broadly as he observed the little flower girls approaching. The congregation was entertained as the twins swept along in their blush-pink dresses with matching floral crowns, looking very precious. They walked down the middle aisle, blowing bubbles from cute vials until they reached the altar.

Alexis's wedding gown, by Mar-Lyn McCann, was crystal-beaded Venetian lace on ruffled organza. Her three-tiered veil looked exquisite, the headpiece of freshwater pearl and crystal in stark contrast to her dark hair styled in an up do. Dante sparkled in a dark pinstriped morning suit and top hat and sporting a blush-pink corsage.

The bride and groom broke with tradition by using separate side aisles as they proceeded individually to the altar. The school orchestra played the wedding march, and as the bridal couple advanced from opposite sides, the cute twin sisters blew bubbles towards each of them, delighting their family and friends.

Lady Tamar and Lord Victor walked with Dante's parents behind bridesmaids Cass and Bianca to the front pews, smiling amongst the bubbles. Judith and Gina were among the choristers from the Alexis College of Music.

When the bridal couple returned, after signing the church register, the orchestra played beautifully light music while six choristers walked towards the sanctuary and stood behind the bride and groom. They looked exquisite in a variety of pastel outfits and smiled demurely as the orchestra accompanied them in their rendition of "Perhaps Love" by John Denver. Their clear voices, like a heavenly choir, with breathtaking harmony, reverberated in the silent Winchester Cathedral.

Alexis and Dante, both touched by the appropriateness of the lyrics, acknowledged their presence by inviting them to join the bridal retinue for the recessional wedding march.

In the courtyard, as Dante's family, colleagues, and friends gathered to congratulate them, Alexis gently beckoned the six choristers and embraced them warmly before turning to her husband. "Dante," she said in a soft voice, "these are my sisters – the beatific choristers."

Alexis's sisters were amazing. They congratulated Dante and his family as if they had known the family for years. Janet and Vince were clearly impressed as they watched their little twin daughters being lovingly embraced by each of Alexis's sisters.

Dante was discreet. "Thanks for coming. We'd like photos with you, if that's—"

But Alexis had slipped away, her heart pounding. *If only these tears would stop,* she thought.

Guests were directed to Sally Park, a few miles from the Consani Village Hotel, where photographs would be taken, followed by drinks and canapés in a giant gazebo at the far end of the park.

A special bridal banquet had been arranged at the hotel. The dining hall looked magnificent, with golden chandeliers and unique oil paintings adorning the walls. The tables were tastefully prepared with crisp linen, gleaming cutlery, and delicate china. Impeccably dressed staff glided between tables, directing guests to their places.

During the delectable five-course meal, Alexis's gaze travelled to the end of the table where her young sisters-in-law were seated. They were engaged in cheerful conversation, without the slightest difference in their regard for their youngest sisters, Bridget and Celine. This touched Alexis deeply, as she recalled her own childhood and how much she had missed out on her sisters' company whenever they talked about girly matters like clothing, hairstyles, boyfriends, and dates.

Meanwhile, her sisters were talking animatedly to Dante's extended family and guests. Her vision blurred as she recalled through her tears the message that Marcia had whispered earlier.

"The twins won't be staying long. Dad's asked them to help organize a surprise birthday celebration for Mum. The rest of us will stay with you – we need to have a chat before you and Dante leave tonight. Everything's been lovely so far."

Marcia had patted her younger sister's hand as she'd blinked back the tears stinging in her eyes. Feelings of rejection were triggered in Alexis, and she struggled to contain her emotions. She withdrew into her private thoughts.

What else will Mum and Dad do to add to my aching heart? The fireworks we'll be having later in the evening – Mum's specialty – were specially chosen to mark her sixtieth birthday. Why do they continue to punish me even on such a momentous occasion? Dad knows how close I've always been to Zoë and Cathy. Why could he not reschedule the celebration when Mum's birthday's only tomorrow? If only they could have been here to share this day with me.

Alexis dabbed at her eyes with tissue and decided to mingle among the guests later, and then she might spend time with her sisters and their husbands. For now, she needed to shelve her pain and enjoy her wedding day. Plucked from dwelling on the past by Dante's warm hand on hers, she said in a quiet voice, "My husband, my best friend, my pillar of support." She smiled at him.

Dante's arm came protectively around her shoulders as he gave her a gentle squeeze and kissed the top of her head. "My wife, my best friend, my pillar of strength. We're going to be master builders of family life. Promise?" He stood up and held out his hand in invitation.

"I promise," she said as they headed towards the dance square for the Viennese Waltz.

CHAPTER 28

As the weeks and months passed, Alexis and Dante began to settle happily into married life and enjoyed being spoilt by the hotel staff in their elaborate suite. They enjoyed tasty meals and special privileges of privacy despite the fact that Bianca and Cass still occupied their own space in the Manor.

Their work in school continued to flourish, as young ladies from all walks of life applied to the Academy with blossoming dreams for their musical talents.

"Dante," Alexis said at the board meeting, "I think we need to consider applying for a subsidy for talented young girls."

"The school's virtually bursting at the seams with growing numbers – we're booked up for two years. Why would you want to pay for more students?" Gloria asked.

"I'm talking about assisting existing students," Alexis explained. "I would not like to see them dropping out due to a lack of funds."

Alexis was determined to arrange subsidies for struggling families who barely managed to afford school fees. "We have many students who are talented at performing but cannot afford to buy their own instruments for their homework practice. With a government subsidy, we could purchase instruments and have students borrow them on a contract basis," she said.

Gloria was concerned. "That's a brilliant idea, but do you need more ladies to join the orchestra, Alexis?"

Gina was irritated. "Haven't you listened to what Alexis proposed? She's talking about students practising with their *own* instruments because what they're using are school property. Reframed, she's talking about encouraging discipline, responsibility, and playing skilfully."

"Precisely! I like the idea very much," Dante said. "Gina, you've hit the nail on the head. This project should shift the onus of practice onto the students and make our load a lot lighter."

Alexis exchanged a smile with her husband. "That's right! Parents will then come on board and support us by encouraging practice as part of their daughters' daily routines."

———✾———

"We have good news," Alexis announced to Bianca and Cass as she and Dante settled down for their six-month anniversary supper.

"Celine and Bridget are going to be aunts, right?" Bianca said excitedly, and she embraced the couple warmly. "I was beginning to wonder when my honorary-aunt status was going to kick in."

Her excitement mounting, Cass discreetly whispered to the headwaiter before returning to embrace the parents-in-waiting. "Congratulations to our mum and dad-to-be! Tell us – is it a boy or a girl?"

Alexis smiled demurely. *How can I tell them that I'd prefer a daughter to nurture, encourage, and guide, especially during those tender years? In fact, I'd like only two children – both girls. That would be sheer bliss.*

"I'd like a son," Dante declared, "and I'd name him after someone I really admire. We've already discussed it, but we'll wait and see before we disclose the name. Alexis hasn't expressed her preference, so I'm sure she wouldn't mind whether it's a son or a daughter." He smiled and touched her cheek tenderly.

The waiter served a special peach drink, and Cass proposed a toast: "To the new family." Alexis giggled as another waiter arrived with a large teddy bear, which he placed in a child's high chair. Two hotel violinists approached, playing, "Congratulations and Celebrations" to the excited young couple, who were clearly thrilled at being cheered and entertained on this significant day – six months away from being parents.

For a while dinner was forgotten, as guests from nearby tables started singing and clapping to the lively rhythm. Dante drew his wife to her feet, and the two danced gracefully, while other couples followed their lead around the dance floor.

———✾———

One morning Cass and Bianca were rustling up a hearty breakfast, but there was an uncomfortable silence before Alexis spoke up.

"I'm not sure we could continue living in the Manor with a baby on the way. Both of you will need your sleep, and our pyjama drill might disturb you – besides all the other demands that babies bring. Maybe Dante and I need to consider having our own apartment."

"Whatever for?" Bianca asked. "Here I am, waiting for my honorary-aunt status to get underway, and you want to deprive me. I always said I would help you, so don't spoil my chances."

"Exactly," Cass said. "I'm looking forward to helping you with the nursery and caring for your precious bundle. You're going to need plenty of rest while Dante's at work."

When Dante reached over and gently touched the hand of his heavily pregnant wife, Cass and Bianca discreetly left the couple in the breakfast nook to enjoy their breakfast. They sensed that the couple probably needed their privacy.

"We will hire a nanny to assist us, honey," Dante said gently, "if that's any consolation to you. And don't worry; we'll break the news when we can arrange to meet both our families."

Alexis did not answer. She was thinking of Bianca and Cass, and in the pit of her stomach was a knot of anxiety. How was she going to juggle her time? Then she remembered her promise to Dante on their wedding night.

She placed her other hand on his. "We will do our best to be good parents, won't we? Please be there for me when I forget my pledge about building up family life. Promise?"

"I promise," he said. "We're both going to learn from the mistakes we witnessed in life."

Dante decided to take matters into his own hands and set the wheels in motion for a family meeting. Alexis deserved only the best, and he would devote his life to caring for her, ensuring that their family life brought her the fulfilment, joy, and love that she'd always craved. This was his personal pledge; his family would be his main focus, just as he remembered experiencing it in his own family.

Janet and Vince found the venue easily, while Bridget and Celine smiled broadly between their older sisters, who seemed puzzled by this mystery drive. Cass and Bianca drove in circles until they spotted Dante's car, and then they parked beside it.

The venue was in Brighton, but it was dark, and they seemed unable to walk any further because of a high wall covered with hessian sacking.

"Hello!" Vince called. "Dante, we're here, son!"

The silence made the darkness seem ominous. Soon there were more voices behind them – unfamiliar and invisible in the darkness. Janet held Bridget and Celine's hands lest they started whining. After much shuffling around and more voices calling *hello,* the lights went on, and everyone applauded as they saw the door opening to a magnificent house. Alexis and Dante emerged, hand in hand, clearly glowing with joy as they appeared in the doorway.

"Welcome to our new home," Dante announced, stepping out and removing the hessian covering from the wall to open the gate. "Now that you know our new address, follow me!"

Everyone was in awe of the tastefully decorated rooms as he led them through the house, until they reached Alexis in the vast lounge. There, round tables contained place cards for every guest.

Alexis's sisters and their families were at one large table. They were all clearly delighted to see their sister's new home. Bianca and Cass automatically took over the catering and ordered Alexis to relax. Everyone shared animatedly about how they had initially struggled before finding their way and then reaching the venue in darkness.

Janet and Vince were seated with Bridget and Celine at the main table, along with Alexis and Dante. They were as charming as they teasingly reproached their son for causing the chaos. The twins looked pleased at being placed between Alexis and their brother, because their new sister-in-law clearly doted on them. The atmosphere was warm and friendly as Alexis eventually rose and tinkled her glass for her guests' attention. Dante stood beside her, holding her hand affectionately.

"We're delighted to let you know that we're twice as happy since we first heard the news of our baby." She paused briefly when she realized that none of her guests quite understood her hidden message. With a gentle nod from Dante, she blurted out, "We're having twins!"

Everyone applauded and cheered, while her sisters and in-laws spontaneously embraced her.

Marcia chose this opportunity to address her sister and brother-in-law on behalf of the family. "Alexis," she said in a quiet voice. "You've come a long way over many years. I've also noticed your grand piano – something you always wanted as a little girl. I hope someone will be playing tonight. I want you to know we're very proud of you." Then, with tears streaming down her cheeks, she continued, "Thank you, Dante, for your endearing nature. Alexis is happy, and we're happy for her. We're so pleased to welcome another brother-in-law." She sat down, smiling through her tears, while Dylan warmly squeezed her hand.

Janet stood behind Marcia, her hands gently touching the younger woman's shoulders.

"Thank you, Marcia, and each member of Alexis's family. We value your presence. The bond of love among you and your respective families is very evident. My son is fortunate to be married to Alexis. He loves her – no, I mean he *adores* her. And we're happy for him.

"We are here tonight to celebrate the imminent birth of two new lives. Let us keep our focus. As for the mother-to-be of my twin grandchildren," she said, smiling at Alexis, "I know you're going to be great, Alexis; I sense that. Bridget and Celine have already asked permission to babysit, so you won't have to worry about nannies."

The twins nodded vigorously, to the amusement of all the guests, while Alexis gave them each a tender squeeze before addressing everyone with a warm and winning smile.

"Thanks, Janet. Bridget and Celine will have lots to teach me. Thanks everyone, for sharing this evening with us. We have lots of catching up to do."

Cathy announced, "Alexis, we'd like you and Dante to sing the song we sang at your wedding."

Alexis smiled and nodded graciously to Cathy. Dante stood beside her as they sang "Perhaps Love" as a duet, accompanied by Marcia on the grand piano. Their families were impressed by their melodic voices and were visibly moved by the couple's occasional smiles to each other and their guests. This song was a Versini favourite, which they often sang on special occasions like birthdays or their parents' wedding anniversary.

Their big brother's singing so impressed Bridget and Celine– they probably thought he only knew rhymes and riddles – that they spontaneously dashed over and stood between the couple, smiling ingenuously.

CHAPTER 29

Dante sighed. He so dearly wanted to give Alexis everything she'd ever wanted as his wife and mother of their children, but he had not expected her reaction to fraternal twins. She seemed set on having twin girls. For a brief moment after the announcement that they had one boy and one girl, it had seemed that she was no longer the woman he'd married. He'd tried to soothe her, thinking it was just a fleeting reaction after the trauma of birth, but she appeared resolute. She only acknowledged their little girl.

"We'll name her after Lady Tamar," Alexis said, smiling at their infant daughter. "Why don't we call her Tamara and abbreviate it to Tara as a pet name?"

"In that case, we'll call our son Victor," Dante said. "That way we'll honour Lady Tamar *and* Victor, who've stood in as your parents and made you a beneficiary."

Then he saw her face brighten. "What about Brigido?" Alexis asked. "We'll call him Brigido. Mum would be pleased, and so would Dad. They could raise him for us," she said, without taking her eyes off Tamara.

"No, Alexis! We'll call him Victor, and Vic will be his pet name. He is our child, and we will raise him together with his sister. Have some rest, love. I'll feed Vic in the nursery from the bottle we've prepared."

Dante removed his shirt and held their little son close to his chest, weeping as he did so. "Vic," he said quietly to his boy, "Mom is very tired, and she needs lots of rest. Daddy will feed you and take care of you. We love you very much; always remember that."

He sat in the rocking chair and held the tiny boy in his arms and watched him feed. Meanwhile, he allowed his tears to flow as he recalled Alexis's hysteria and how she had turned her back on their son when she'd first laid eyes on him.

He had seen their son's body stiffen around his shoulder while he was holding him during Alexis's loud outburst. Dante wondered whether little Vic felt afraid or anxious during his mother's ranting and raving when she expressed her preference for his little sister.

While feeding Victor from his bottle, Dante recalled the story Alexis had told him about her childhood, being raised as a boy and how much she resented it. Could she be projecting her anger and pain towards her father onto their son? Is that why she wanted him to be called Brigido? He dearly hoped little Victor wasn't going to be the scapegoat for all of Alexis's pent-up emotions.

"Please, God," Dante pleaded, crying softly, his heart aching with sorrow and confusion. "Soften Alexis's heart, and help her to love our son too. He's innocent and deserves as much love as our little Tara. Guide me as a husband and father to do what is right by Alexis and our beautiful children. Thanks for their health; thanks for giving them to us. Please teach us how to love both our babies, God." He sobbed for their little boy, who had dozed off. Alexis had decided not to breastfeed their son, saying that she did not have the physical energy to feed two babies.

Dante placed the sleeping infant into his Moses basket and returned to the main bedroom, where he found Alexis fast asleep and little Tara whimpering. He lifted his little girl into his arms and held her gently, rocking her to and fro. He recalled how he'd felt the same tenderness when he'd held his twin sisters nearly seven years ago. Although he had declared his preference for a son, he did not love one of his children over the other. He loved them both.

"Dante," Alexis whispered when she awoke and watched him with their daughter, "isn't she beautiful?"

She looked into his eyes, a dazzling smile lighting up her face, and he felt his heart somersaulting. Maybe Alexis hadn't changed as much as he'd thought.

"Yes, darling, she's even more beautiful when she's asleep. I'm going to put her down to rest with her brother. They've probably missed each other, having grown together for nine months. They need their rest. Let's go to the morning room. Benita will see to them when they waken, and Harold's arranged breakfast for us – not sure about you, but I'm famished. You need to regain your strength, honey.

———❖———

Benita was the twins' nanny, and Harold took charge of domestic chores with aplomb. Both of them had vast experience with childcare and household tasks. Dante knew their children were in safe hands.

The crackling fire in the morning room was warm and welcoming as Alexis and Dante settled down to an English breakfast. Alexis was looking herself again, and Dante decided to broach the subject he'd been longing to discuss with her.

"Alexis, how would you feel about working for the Academy from home? You could be doing some of the paperwork for the Bursary Fund during your break for caring for Tara and Vic, until you're ready to return full time."

"I could do more, like coaching instrumentals and preparing students for orchestral concerts."

"Please, I don't want you exerting yourself, honey. Remember: our home is our private space, and having students around might encroach on our personal lives."

"I never thought of that, but you're right. Maybe I could focus on preparing for concerts, then."

Dante's face was filled with rapture as he recognized that he had his wife back. She seemed to be herself again. Her desire to return to work in six months' time and leave their children in professional care was a good sign.

The door opened, and quite unexpectedly Bridget and Celine breezed into the room and planted kisses on their brother and his wife before making their predictable request. "We've come to offer our help with the babies," Celine said. "I want to hold Tamara, and my sister wants to hold Victor. Our mid-term break starts tomorrow, and we want to organize our time."

Dante's mouth had begun to twitch uncontrollably at the thought of his darling little sisters taking over the nursery, and as he caught Alexis's eye, she too was stifling a giggle.

"Come and sit here first," Alexis said, inviting the twins to sit on her lap. "I haven't seen you for ages."

Dante scooped Bridget into his arms and tickled her affectionately. She was the shyer twin and more observant than Celine. From day one he had longed to find out her rationale for choosing Vic over Tara. Bridget also spoke less than her sister, having become more conscious of her lisp since starting primary school. Although Celine was her closest ally and obviously her best antidote, she loved sharing secrets with her big brother.

"So you've fallen in love with Vic, have you?" Dante asked. "No wonder you want to help."

Bridget spoke in a soft voice. "I'm not in love; I juth love him very muth, cauth he'th very thpethial, cauth boyth don't alwayth have fun like girlth with nithe clotheth and thtuff. Tho if we love him more, hith clotheth won't be tho important."

Dante was touched by his little sister's empathy and held her very close. Alexis and Celine were engrossed in their own conversation and missed what Bridget had just disclosed, but Dante felt reassured that his son had an aunt who would look out for him.

"Let's go and see if they're still sleeping, shall we?" Dante took her hand and led her to the nursery.

Vic was still fast asleep when they entered, but Tara had just woken up, and Benita was there, ready to attend to her needs. Bridget was very excited and ran to greet her little niece.

"Hello, my baby," Alexis said as she stepped in and took Tara from Benita. "See to him when he wakes up," she said to Benita, nodding towards Victor. "Come, Princess, Mommy's here to take care of you. Come along, girls, I need your help. Benita, be a dear and bring her bath water."

Vic woke up half an hour later, and Benita brought him to his mother. "Would you like to give him a bath as well, Mrs Campbell?"

"Not now, Benita. Please see to him, my dear," Alexis said sweetly. "I can't leave Tara with the girls. They're still very little. When you've given him his bath, you could bring him here and the girls could hold a baby each. We'd like to take photos with them, wouldn't we, girls?"

"Yes!" they said in unison, looking excited. Bridget, however, wanted to follow Benita, but Alexis called after her. "Bridget, come and hold Tara while Celine helps me to tidy up.

Benita will bring Vic when he's ready." She patted the bed for Bridget to sit and hold her little niece.

Meanwhile, Dante headed off to the stores to do some grocery shopping with Harold.

———❀———

"Dinner is served, Mrs Campbell!" Harold invited. "Mr Campbell says Bridget and Celine need to practise their music pieces after lunch," he added.

"That's fine, Harold!" Alexis said. "Come along, girls; let's go and have dinner." She carried Tamara with her to the dining room.

Dante was on hand to assist Harold with the dishes from the kitchen. He knew about his sisters' poor appetite, so he encouraged them caringly. "Bridget and Celine, if you want to help us with the babies, you're going to have to build up your muscles and eat properly from now on, OK?"

The girls nodded vigorously, until they spotted Benita bringing Vic, and then they promptly left their seats to rally around her. They vied for Vic's attention, forgetting their promise to their big brother.

"Dante, there's Vic!" Celine exclaimed excitedly. "May I hold him after dinner, please?"

Alexis was firm. "Girls, you've just promised to build up strong muscles. Have your dinner, and you'll have more time with the babies afterwards. Benita will see to Vic. He's getting very heavy for little girls to carry. I'll place him on your lap when you're sitting on the bed, OK?"

"Honey, why don't we let Benita take Tara as well, and then you can have your dinner in peace," Dante suggested.

"I've had a good breakfast, dear," Alexis said. "Benita could accompany the girls for a walk. It's so lovely outside. After that, girls, you will need to have your music practice. Benita will keep an eye on you, won't you dear?"

"Certainly, Mrs Campbell," Benita said. "Vitamin D is very good for the skin."

"Dante," Alexis said, suddenly changing the subject while holding Tara firmly. "Why don't we decide on the instruments we intend purchasing, go through the list of students we've earmarked, and draw up contracts for their parents?"

"Sounds brilliant, honey! We could also decide on the repertoire for the orchestra so that there'd be ample time for the concert and our Christmas pageant."

Within a few weeks Alexis and Dante had arranged interviews with the parents of the twenty students they had chosen, to discuss contracts for the care of instruments and regular daily practice.

CHAPTER 30

Alexis basked in the early evening sunshine, smiling serenely, with Tara fast asleep in her arms. She was pleased with the progress her babies were making. Benita and Harold had proven to be very capable with the twins and the household chores. The few sessions of Pilates had already settled her physique and helped her get back into shape. She looked forward to the time when she would return to the Academy and resume her position in the music department.

"Honey, Marcia's on the line; she wants to come over and visit," Dante announced that Saturday evening.

"I'm going for a shower, Dante," Alexis said. "Attend to her, please! I'll be as quick as I can."

"Marcia, come on over," Dante said. "By the time you arrive, she'll be all set and ready. Yes, of course, bring your husband and children. We'd love to have them over as well. No, you don't need to bring anything along. Just come!"

Alexis had blow-dried her hair and slipped into a metallic pleated skirt and cotton blouse by the time Harold received Marcia and her family at the door.

"Good evening, Alexis. You're look stunning in that outfit," her sister said. "Girls, come and say hello to Aunt Alexis and Uncle Dante. Dylan's just met a friend in the parking bay – he'll be here in a minute."

"Lovely to see you, girls. My, look how you've grown! Are either of you following in your mom's footsteps with music?" Alexis asked.

"Mom and Dad are too busy in the bridal shop. But I'm enjoying my music classes," the older one said.

"'Bridal shop'? What do you mean? Marcia, have you not kept up with your music?"

"No time, Alexis," Marcia said. "Girls, why don't you wait for Daddy, while Mommy and Aunt Alexis speak in private." The girls quietly stepped into the hallway.

Marcia spoke in a hushed tone. "I took a stand, Alexis. I refused to have anything more to do with music until Dad mended his ways. Dylan only works part time at his architecture, and otherwise he works with me. Initially it was a struggle, but our bridal shop, Mar-Lyn McCann is thriving, because marriage is becoming more and more popular."

"Mar-Lyn McCann?" But that's where I bought my wedding gown!" Alexis said. "I didn't see either of you there."

"Really? Oh, Alexis, I'm so thrilled. I thought your dress looked familiar. Dylan and I were away for the summer holiday with the girls when you came. In fact, Candice mentioned that she thought she recognized you when you came for the final fitting, but she felt shy, because you had an elderly couple along with you. She thought she was mistaken."

"Yes, that's right. Lady Tamar and Lord Victor were with me. What a pity that Candice did not approach me."

"Like I said, she felt shy, and generally, the working staff do not socialize with customers."

"Of course, but how is she doing, Marcia? I know she's done dress designing, but is she permanently employed?"

"Yes, she's one of my top designers – there are three others working with her. She's an excellent seamstress, and she sews most of our wedding gowns."

"Oh wow!" Alexis exclaimed. "What about a family? Does she have a family?"

"Yes, her daughter, Justine, had just started high school when her husband passed away."

"Justine? Is her daughter's name Justine Samuels?" Alexis was ecstatic.

"That's right," Marcia said. "She married Justin Samuels, but he had a tragic accident two years ago, leaving her with three daughters. The younger two are still in primary school."

"Dante and I have chosen Justine Samuels for a scholarship, and we're supposed to interview her parents in due course. What a surprise! That's the best news – I must tell Bianca and Cass. What a small world! Please tell her that I've asked about her and that I'd like us to meet."

"Certainly! Alexis, do you realize that you've also chosen my daughters?" Marcia said gently as she removed the letter from her handbag and showed it to her sister.

"Dante," Alexis called and smiled as he entered the room with Dylan and his daughters. "This was your idea, wasn't it?" she said, smiling proudly. "My darlings," Alexis said, addressing her nieces. "If you're ready for hard work in the Academy, Uncle Dante and I will give you all the support you need."

The girls bounced with excitement as they spontaneously hugged their aunt and uncle.

"So we *will* be having music in our home, after all," Dylan said, winking at his wife.

"Thanks, Alexis and Dante," Marcia said. It looked as if someone had flicked on a light switch inside her face.

The day of their first rehearsal dawned, and the music hall was buzzing with teenagers excited to be in the thirty-six-seat auditorium. By mid-afternoon, Alexis arrived for the new junior orchestra.

Dante announced the various sections and then the names of students playing specific instruments and their seating positions.

"Ladies, I am going to address you by the section you're in; for example, the woodwind section comprises clarinets, bassoons, double bassoons, piccolos, flutes, and oboes. The string section includes the harp, first and second violins, violas, cello, double bass, and so forth. Are you ready?"

"Yes, Mrs Campbell!" they exclaimed excitedly.

Alexis singled out each section, pausing between each: "Percussion! … brass! … woodwind! … piano! … strings!"

"Eye contact is important. Wait for your cue, listen to each other, and … focus!"

They nodded.

The orchestra played as one, and Alexis's eyes blurred as she caught sight of Justine, Claire, and Cherie, in the string section, adding to the splendour of "The Phantom of the Opera".

Bianca, Cass, and Candice attended the rehearsal, and Dylan captured the electric moment on camera.

CHAPTER 31

W hen the twins were two-and-a-half years of age, it had become more and more apparent that Vic was the quiet twin, while his sister, Tara, was more confident and clearly the apple of her mother's eye. Then Dante started noticing his son's interest in music, and watched him toddle over to the grand piano whenever he had a chance.

He placed Victor on his lap. "You want Daddy to play for you?" he asked and placed his son's hands on top of his while he played a simple tune.

Vic pushed his dad's hands away and replicated the piece of music. Dante was astounded. His little son was a genius, to be able to play that piece without having had a single lesson.

"Alexis," he called, leaving his son to play on his own. "Alexis, come and see this. Vic is playing the grand piano!"

"Tara, come with Mommy," she called and followed Dante to the lounge. "Dante, why's he at the piano when he has his own toys?"

"Haven't you heard what I just said, Alexis?" Dante was agitated. "This child plays pieces on his own. He's probably shy now, but I swear I heard him playing. You know the piece I played last night, "I'm So Pretty", from *Westside Story*? I found it quite difficult to play initially, but Vic played it after I did ... it's amazing! Our son's got talent, and he needs to develop it, Alexis! He plays from memory."

Dante watched his son smiling shyly at Tara and said, "Vic, show Mommy and Tara how well you can play. Come along, buddy!"

But Vic climbed down and started whining. His dad picked him up, and there were tears in his eyes as he realized that his son was a genius and already lacking the confidence to play in his own home. Dante decided that even at this tender age, his son was not too young to be mentored. He would have to devise a plan.

Days later, Dante noticed that his son was listening to the music on his car radio and whenever anyone spoke, he'd cock his head in the direction of the speakers to listen more carefully.

Dante attempted for the umpteenth time, "Vic, count for Daddy, 1-2-3, 1-2-3," but the little chap seemed uninterested in his dad's theory lesson. He just wanted to play.

When he approached the lounge one evening, Dante found Vic at the piano and Tara dancing to the music he played. He was stunned. His son was playing the very music he had heard on the car radio. He felt a cold sweat on his neck and back when he realized that Vic had a natural musical talent. This was beyond him – his son needed someone more professional. Nothing was going to stop him from giving his son the very best tuition. He discussed his plans about private tuition with Alexis and asked her opinion.

"By all means," Alexis said. "But I think Boys' Academy will be our best option, because he will be among other talented children. It's a boarding school, and he'll grow in confidence. With his timid nature, he could easily be bullied in a regular school. He only plays for his sister but not when his namesake Victor visits us. But I'm sure he'll do well in the boys' choir and develop his musical skills among the other boys."

"I don't like the idea of a boarding school, Alexis," Dante said. "I've had a word with Professor Keanan, and he shared some important insights with me."

"Dante," she interrupted, "I attended boarding school for five years, and I've come out tops. Today I'm one of the only female conductors in the country!"

Your parents rejected you, Dante thought. *I will not let my son go through what your parents put you through. He shares your musical talent, no doubt, but he will not be subjected to the same treatment you've been through. Not now, not ever. We love our little boy, and we don't need to leave our home to pursue his talent without giving him the best support we can. He's still a baby. I'll take some advice and coach him until he's ready for pre-primary schooling.*

"Alexis, that was high school, and you had a family who visited you regularly and supported you in your giftedness. Vic obviously takes after you, and we need to nurture his talents without depriving him of emotional and physical support. He's far too young to be left in a boarding school."

"Times are different," she said. "Why don't we enrol him early to avoid disappointment? We'll definitely pay our way and support him, as you suggest."

"According to Professor Keanan, he's a born musician but far too young for boarding school. He's of the opinion that Vic is ready to perform in an orchestra, but only with lots of support. He just needs to listen to pieces, practise them, and then play."

"Let's see what he's like with strings," Alexis said. "See if he'll play the violin, cello, or viola."

Dante took his son to the family's music room and saw his face light up when he opened the cases to reveal the cello, violin, and viola in separate cases. The child was overjoyed.

"Oh wow!" Vic exclaimed. "Is this Bidget's violin?" he said enthusiastically while carefully stroking the violin his dad handed to him. It was as though Vic came to life when he instinctively positioned the instrument and held the bow, ready to play.

"Listen, buddy, this is not Bridget's violin," Dante said. "Daddy and Mommy are giving you permission to play any one of these instruments. You're not to let your friends come in here and play with them – they're not toys!"

"OK, Dad!" Vic's face shone with excitement as he nodded, waiting for an opportunity to play. Dante smiled as he watched his son playing despite his struggle to hold the instrument in position. He played tricky musical pieces with ease. Admiring his tenacity, Dante decided to search online for smaller instruments and invest in string instruments for his son to manage and master.

CHAPTER 32

"I still think boarding school will do him good, Dante," Alexis said. "He'll have more supervision with his music. We both know what practice involves, but with our household, grading of work, preparing our lessons, and caring for our daughter, we won't do justice to his giftedness. He needs friendships and socializing with peers, which is what he'll have when he's at the Boys' Academy. Besides that, Dante, Tara needs to develop her gifts too."

"That's true. Why don't we talk to him about it? He needs to know that we love him and that we want him to pursue his gift of music."

"Good idea, but don't beg him, please, Dante. We're his parents, and we know what's good for him. Just tell him, and be the parent."

"I agree that we know what's good for him, Alexis, but we also need to listen to him. I don't want our son growing up as a wimp – someone without a backbone. He will obey if he understands our rationale and has a few choices of his own to make."

"If that's what you believe, then go ahead. Speak to him and listen to what he says. I'll leave that to you."

"No, Alexis," Dante said. "He needs reassurance from you as his mother, and we need to be in this together. Vic needs to hear encouragement from both of us."

"But you're the head of the home, Dante," she said. "I don't need to speak as well – if he's that genius, he'll understand quicker, won't he? You talk to him, and I'll stand by your decision."

Dante felt very uneasy. "Alexis, we've agreed that we're going to stand together as a family. In this case, it's important for Vic to see that you and I are united in our decision here. We'll have to speak to the nursery school principal as well, because Vic will need to exit soon."

"I've just agreed with you, Dante. What more do you want?" Alexis looked vulnerable, and there was a tremor in her voice. "We're going to spend money on instruments, private tuition, and extra classes because of his age. Tara's not going to get any of this – and you want me to speak to him with or after you. Is that going to be the case every time you decide to speak to either of our children, that both of us have to be present? Is that how you were raised, Dante? I'm going outside to be with our daughter. How must she feel – nothing's being done for her. It's all about Vic, but our daughter has to go to a regular preschool next year and miss out on being with her brother."

"Why don't we speak to both of them," Dante suggested. "Let's explain why Vic will attend Boys' Academy. In that way we'll encourage Tara to support her brother."

Alexis was delighted. "All right. You do the talking, and I'll fill in whatever I think needs to be said. But remember to reassure Tara as well – she'll be at home while he's enjoying life."

The twins were playing in the garden, and Alexis suggested that Dante broach the subject right where they were. She nodded to Dante and placed Vic on her lap, while he held Tara.

"Buddy," Dante addressed his son. "Mommy and Daddy know how much you like to play the piano—"

"And he plays the violin," Tara interjected.

"That's right; he also plays the violin," Dante said with a big smile, winking at Alexis.

"Vic," Alexis asked gently, "how would you like to go to a special school and learn more about playing the piano and the violin?"

"Oh wow!" he said, his face lighting up. "A big school like Bidget and Celine?"

"Something like that", Dante explained, "but not quite the same. You'll be with boys, and you will have lots of time to practise your music on your own and with the other boys."

"Will Tara come too?" he asked thoughtfully, a tear slipping down his cheek. "She can come draw in my school."

Dante was touched by his son's observation and his caring

manner of including his sister. "That's true – you like drawing, don't you, Princess?" he said.

She smiled broadly. "I have lots of drawings for my brother."

"Dante," Alexis said. "Before I download application forms for Vic, I thought Tara could do creative dancing. She's at the right age to start, and she has the aptitude and physique."

"Sounds wonderful, honey. Go ahead with the application forms for Vic, but let's hear what our princess says." He turned to Tara, "Is that what you would like to do, Princess? Learn ballet?"

Tara nodded. "Will Vic be at my school, Daddy?"

"No, Princess, Vic will be at a different school. He will sleep there and come home for visits. Are you listening, buddy? We will visit you every Sunday and attend all your concerts."

Vic appeared dismissive. "Do I have to take all my clothes and my superman pyjamas and my bike and my birthday presents?"

"Mommy will pack for you, buddy," Dante said, smiling affectionately. "But you may add anything that Mom forgets."

Alexis's feelings of irritation towards Dante were eclipsed by her excitement to enrol Tara into such a splendid dancing school. She was determined to give her daughter every opportunity to excel at dancing.

"How many sleeps for my school, Daddy?" Victor sounded excited.

"And how many sleeps for my school?" Tara echoed, looking very serious.

Dante lifted the twins onto his knees. They held each other affectionately while their dad dandled them on his knees. "Whoa! Run faster, ponies, Mom and Dad are waiting for you. Hurry up!"

The children were squealing with delight when Alexis returned with a tray carrying fruit juices and smiling broadly. "That wasn't so difficult, was it? Vic seemed quite all right about boarding school," Alexis said.

"You're right; I was surprised too. We'll still need to keep an eye though. He loves music, that's for sure, but to separate the twins is quite tough for me to accept at the moment. I suppose he'll toughen up and be more focused. I mustn't be selfish."

"Dante, will you complete the forms online and fill in a date for the interview? I think it might be better if you attended the auditioning session with Vic, and I'll see to matters at school."

"We'll go together, Alexis! For now, let's have a cup of tea!"

CHAPTER 33

Dante and Alexis accompanied their son to the Boys' Academy. They abided by the rules of the Academy which asked them not to prepare their son with ear tests and extra coaching. Dante had the quiet confidence that Vic was going to master the auditions. In his own music background and experience, he had singled out one or two musical geniuses, but with his own son falling into this category, it was awesome.

"Good morning, young man. My name is Miss McGuire," the receptionist said. "What's yours?"

"Good morning; my name is Victor Campbell."

"You're as cute as a button in your dark trousers, fancy white shirt, and bow tie. Come along!"

"Thank you, Miss McGuire," he said as he took her extended hand, and he and his parents accompanied her to the audition hall. Mignon, one of the panellists, crouched in front of Vic and gave him an instruction before asking him to take his position in front of the desk.

Dante felt relaxed, but Alexis could barely disguise her amazement when their little boy played "Annie's Song" by John Denver on his violin. But they felt anxious when they noticed the blank expressions of the interviewing panel. Victor then played "Tonight" from *West Side Story* on the piano followed by "Memory" from the musical *Cats* on the viola. After his audition, Vic rested the instruments on the bench behind him, placed both hands on one hip, and sat down.

"Victor Campbell, that was well done! Please take a seat in the foyer," Miss McGuire announced in a warm and friendly tone. When he didn't move, she repeated herself, "Thank you, Victor; you may wait in the foyer."

Dante, feeling embarrassed at his son's tardiness, stepped forward to fetch his son. "Come along, buddy!" The little boy appeared unresponsive; his face was pale, and he was still holding his side with both hands.

"Come along, Vic!" Alexis said, but when she tried to take his hand, the boy looked very unwell and started retching.

Dante panicked. "Please, somebody, there's something wrong – my boy is ill! Quick, call an ambulance!" Vic looked lethargic and was swaying on his feet, so Dante picked him up.

The paramedics arrived within minutes, and Dante accompanied them to the hospital. The panel was stunned by this turn of events and expressed their concern for the child and his parents. They promised to communicate their decision in due course. Alexis left Tara with Marcia and drove to the hospital to wait with Dante.

The doctor looked stern when he called Dante and Alexis to his office. He told them that their child must have been in terrific pain. They had removed his appendix, but they were amazed that Vic had not complained about pain. According to the doctor, this was most unusual for such a young child – and quite worrying.

Dante spoke in a low voice. "He's had an audition at the Boys' Academy this morning, and that's probably why he didn't tell us. He loves music, and he played exceptionally well today."

"That's probably it, then," the doctor said. "God must have a higher purpose for this child; he could have died today. His appendix was near bursting point. However, he will be discharged within three days – he's a smart kid."

Victor's performance was highly commended, and his acceptance to the Boys' Academy of Music was unanimous. Because of the rigorous training involved at the Academy, the little boy was to be trained in the privacy of his home by a tutor. At six, he would be allowed full-time attendance; meanwhile, they encouraged more time with his parents and family.

Bridget and Celine were in awe of their little nephew, who played from memory after hearing a piece of music only once or twice. Vic was such an incentive to his aunts that the little rascals started calling him *uncle* – though neither of them needed reminders about music practices anymore.

By six years of age, Victor had mastered three string instruments, and Tara was his biggest supporter.

CHAPTER 34

Tara was five years into creative dancing, and her extracurricular components included ballet, ballroom, and tap-dancing. Her wardrobe had grown extensively, with a variety of costumes, shoes, and accessories, because Alexis continued buying only the very best for her. She had huge dreams for Tara and never missed an opportunity to watch her going through her paces.

Every morning Alexis rose early for the routine she had developed for the new academic year: a brisk walk, shower, dressing, and then breakfast with Dante. Tara requested breakfast with her best friend, Julie, after which they would travel together on the school bus. The girls were inseparable, and Alexis admired their relationship. Alexis casually informed Dante of this one evening when they were in their bedroom, but he baulked at the idea. "What makes our daughter want to have breakfast next door, Alexis? Am I expected to agree with this?" He closed the bedroom door, determined to discuss this so he could understand what was going on with their daughter.

"She's not a baby," Alexis raged. "We need to trust her and allow her freedom. There's nobody her age in this house, so she probably just wants the company of someone her age."

Dante virtually matched her tone. "This happens to be her family. Vic's at boarding school, and that's why they're separated. When do we train her to accept her family as it is?"

"How come we accept phases our students go through when they're laid-back, but we don't listen to our daughter? Besides, what will your disagreement do to my word in this house?"

Dante compromised. "You're right. I'm sorry, but next time when either of our children make a request outside of our house rules, please discuss them with me as well. Do we know what

Julie's parents think of this?" He made a mental note to pop next door and speak to her parents.

Alexis was quietly absorbed in her own thoughts. *My daughter will not be treated like a prisoner in our home. I will see to it. She will get whatever she wants from me, no matter what. I'm proud of her, and I will tell her this every day for as long as I live. I won't allow myself to be drawn into agreeing with her father the way my parents did under the guise of loyalty. Tara has been so withdrawn, but since I've allowed her this, she's been much happier. She will have my support at all times.*

Dante broke the silence. "Alexis, will you fetch the girls after school and monitor Tara's afternoon schedule? I'll travel back with Stephen; he's only two doors away and always offers to help out whenever he can."

She kissed his cheek. "Sure, honey; sounds like a good idea," she said, and she slipped under the duvet.

"Dante, one of these days we might have to open our own dance studio," Alexis remarked at breakfast.

"So I've noticed, with all the comings and goings in the spare room over weekends. I'm so glad we've decided to keep that carpet in there," he said, smiling, as he buttered a slice of toast. "I remember Verushkah and Anoushkah's practice days at home. My dad used to plug his ears, and then he'd ask them in his sweetest voice how long they still had to rehearse."

Alexis chuckled. "The dance sequences Tara teaches are a lot lighter, especially the line dancing. It's not easy teaching a group, but she has tremendous patience and stamina. She insists on good posture – something I wish I could have done at her age. She oozes with self-confidence, that girl. Thankfully she also helps other girls fulfil their dancing dreams."

Dante frowned as if Alexis's words had stumped him. "Whoa, Alexis! Sounds more like *your* unfulfilled dreams come true."

"Yeah, I suppose it is fulfilling to see my daughter doing something I always wanted – so I think we need to encourage her more. Maybe you could also reassure her, Dante!"

"I barely see her, Alexis! In fact, I find her quite withdrawn at times, but when I tease her she laughs, and that gives me a lift just seeing her happy.

"By the way, the twins' milestone birthday is around the corner – we're about to become parents of teenagers, Alexis. Now, that's something to celebrate with the family!"

Her face coloured as she escaped into her thoughts again. *There's no way I'll invite my family over. They're always comparing the twins with each other – making such a fuss of Vic and leaving poor Tara on the sidelines. I'll have none of that.*

If I want to shower my daughter with the love and attention she deserves, so be it. She'll be involved in anything she desires – though I'm glad I've talked her out of those art classes – so bourgeois! I prefer more culturally uplifting activities for her. Vic could learn to draw; his biology sketches are awful. I'll bet Tara would do a better job at it. She's such a talented child.

The *whoosh* of the dishwasher brought Alexis back from her reverie. "Let's not impose our agenda by inviting the family," she said. "I don't want to encourage unhealthy competition between our children. Let them invite their friends to their celebration. You and I can hover around."

"They're not competing – they adore each other! The fact is, they're great together." Dante gave her his megawatt smile. "Like our colleagues say about us at school." He stole a glance at her and saw a sad glint in her eyes; she was apparently ignoring his last comment.

Alexis packed their sandwiches before tidying the kitchen. "Speaking about family, whenever Bridget and Celine visit over a weekends, Tara takes them for dance classes too. Benita asked that her girls also learn, because she couldn't afford the tuition fees. Tara doesn't mind. Reminds me of how I used to help my friends."

Dante carried their attaché cases to the car and activated the driveway gate. "You were an exceptional student, Alexis. Highly motivated, brilliant, and multitalented. Yes, Tara is so much like you, though I think Victor takes after you musically. He's a genius, like you—"

"No!" Alexis interrupted vehemently, causing Dante to look at her in surprise. "I think *Tara's* more like me. I taught Bianca, Candice, and Cass virtually every weekend. Look how close we still are today – devoted and loyal. Tara won't always have us, but she'll have her girlfriends. That's for sure."

Victor like me, my foot! Alexis thought. *What a relief to have him at boarding school, so we can have some peace.*

CHAPTER 35

Dante had the car idling while he waited for Alexis. He thought something was amiss but was unsure. He wanted to get to the bottom of things – perhaps he'd try a different angle. This emphasis on Tara's dancing was becoming too much for him. He felt concerned.

"It's nice that Tara's willing to teach others, but Benita has *five* daughters, Alexis. If she only works here on Saturdays, when will they all learn dancing? Are we responsible for them too? When does Tara take a break, do her homework, study, and simply relax?

"Dancing relaxes her. She told me she does her homework at school. I've seen her studying. We need to show that we trust her. Nobody reminded me to work … nobody cared." Her voice cracked, and Dante noticed tears streaming down her cheeks. He touched her hand gently, but she removed it and held her face in both hands, sobbing. He allowed his wife to weep as he drove in the direction of their favourite Coffee Corner and parked outside. This seemed a good time to alert the secretary that they would be delayed in order to settle a family concern.

Turning to Alexis, he held her gently and felt her body heaving as she sobbed on his shoulder. She had not wept like this in years; he wondered what had brought it on. He dearly wanted her to express her emotions. Her passive-aggressive behaviour lately had become very disturbing to him.

A little while later, Alexis seemed composed as she sat opposite Dante, enjoying her coffee. "Do you remember what the headmistress once said about Tara's low self-esteem? Well, the dancing's helping her. She helps other girls grow in confidence. You should see how well she manages them."

Dante tried to figure out why Alexis was so focused on Tara's dancing and her teaching several girls to dance. He wished he knew how to convince his loving wife of his intention to see his daughter less obsessed with dancing and more engaged in activities that were more age-appropriate. At this rate, she'd be more stressed than her parents.

He spoke gently. "Honey, all I want for our daughter is her happiness, because there's more to life than dancing. I want her to do things *she* enjoys and have a break from school. When does she go to the mall, do clothes shopping, see movies, play hopscotch or tennis, and do something that's outdoors? She needs to socialize with different friends – also boys her age."

There was a tremor in Alexis's voice, and her cheeks trembled with emotion. "I buy her clothes online, Dante; it's the way things are done these days. Tara's a bit young to make choices about her clothes. Young people go after labels instead of good quality. I want to rear her as a lady, not have her wearing some of the torn clothes that teenagers clamour for these days."

"Alexis, do you realize how Vic spends his weekends with us? He practises his music, does homework, and helps me, either in the garage or the garden. Then, of course" – Dante chuckled – "so typically like me, he'll ask for pocket money and go out. We allow this, and that's how he's grown so confident, disciplined, warm, and sociable. They're so close, those two. His weekends could include his sister – they adore each other, Alexis."

Alexis smiled, but her mind was far away. She could hardly wait to meet her daughter after school.

There was freshness in the air after the rain as Alexis waited for Tara and Julie after school. She usually waited no more than five minutes before the lithe little frame came bounding towards the car, followed by her lanky friend. After half an hour, Alexis walked over to the principal's office to inquire about the girls. She felt anxious, because Tara had never kept her waiting.

"Thanks for taking time out of your busy schedule to see me," the headmistress said. "I've told Tara's homeroom teacher that if you don't respond to our third letter—"

"Letter? What are you talking about?" Alexis interjected. "I check my emails every evening."

"They were not emails, Mrs Campbell; it was an official letter from the school."

"Mrs Knight, I came to find out what's keeping Tara and her

friend Julie. Today's her early day, creative dance classes are tomorrow, and on Thursday we've arranged for her to stay with her godmother for the next week or so before the concert. She usually hands me all correspondence from the school, so I don't really know what you're on about."

"Mrs Campbell, Tara has *not* attended dance classes this semester. She sleeps in class, doesn't study, has missed literature tutorials, her grades are down – we're concerned."

"Concerned? Oh really? The semester started several weeks ago, and you tell me of your concerns *today*?" Just then her mobile rang. "Excuse me, Mrs Knight." She stepped out of the room to answer it.

"Bianca, I'm in the principal's office. Please ask Dante to come to the school – yes, please fetch Tara."

Mrs Knight rose, removed a file from her cabinet, and peered over her glasses as Alexis returned. "When the school psychologist spoke to Tara, she broke down and wept for over an hour. Of course, we have not heard what the tears were about – she's highly professional. And according to the school nurse," she continued, "Tara is incredibly underweight. Her homeroom teacher says she's one of our top students, but she's unsure why Tara's not been handing in assignments lately. She's also not bringing sandwiches to school – no fruit or juice. She's become such a sad little person virtually overnight."

Alexis's tears of anger flowed down her cheeks as she absorbed the shocking information. "School psychologist? Who authorized this? You couldn't call my husband or me, but you contacted the school psychologist – and now you give me that drivel about the length of time that my daughter was crying? Is the psychologist also a timekeeper? And are you sure you don't know what Tara said, or were you the one timing her?

"Speaking about *professional*, why does the school nurse report to the headmistress and not the parents? If I hadn't come looking for my daughter today, I would not have been the wiser. Do you pay her school fees? I'll be seeking legal advice, Mrs Knight, just that you know. I've heard enough."

The headmistress nodded thoughtfully. "Let's be reasonable, Mrs Campbell, and address the matter as adults."

"Have you heard what I just said? Have you made *adult* decisions that included us? You have this *huge* file in front of you. Do you not have all our contact details? Who authorized you to make such high-handed decisions about my daughter and draw your own conclusions?"

"I acted in Tara's best interests, Mrs Campbell. She's a good student. We wanted to help."

"That might be so, but your first port of call in the case of a minor is to contact the parents. Leave us to make decisions and find solutions for our children. No wonder Tara cried when she met the school psychologist. Do you know how children view psychologists?"

"Oh absolutely! They think psychologists are for the mentally unstable, but we need to disprove—"

"For goodness' sake – you don't get it, do you? This is ludicrous!" While Alexis was mopping her brow, a text bleeped through on her phone. She wiped the corners of her eyes, her body trembling as she spoke, "Mrs Knight, I ... please ... could you ..."

The headmistress was concerned. "Mrs Campbell! Is there something wrong?"

"Yes. Well, maybe!" She gasped, doubling over, her hands clutching her chest as she tried to ease herself into a chair.

Mrs Knight signalled her receptionist to call for emergency services when she noticed Alexis still holding her chest and not responding to her mobile.

Meanwhile, Bianca organized a lift for Julie and took Tara home. She usually enjoyed her god-daughter's company and looked forward to spending time with her. Hopefully she'd have a break from her dancing sessions and go shopping for the school prom.

Mrs Knight paced up and down as she waited for Dante to arrive. *If only I'd heard about Tara's drop in performance a few days earlier. I might have to start giving the staff verbal warnings; Tara's homeroom teacher has been too tardy. Mrs Campbell's right – had she not come to find out why Tara was delayed, she'd have remained in the dark. I hope the Campbells won't go to the media. Please, God, they're accomplished musicians and highly regarded in the community. I should have followed my hunch and inquired earlier about Tara's gaunt frame; all this could have been prevented. If the school board gets to hear this, they'll be relentless about communication and admonish management.*

The warning about a legal route troubled Mrs Knight, leading to feelings of guilt, confusion, embarrassment, shame, and anger. She planned to summon the staff; she was determined to exercise her authority.

———— ❊ ————

Dante knelt in front of Alexis and held her closely. Her speech was incoherent, her face appeared cool, her lips were purplish, and her clothes were dishevelled. This was not the woman he had kissed goodbye in the morning – this was a stranger. He was just in time to catch Alexis as she collapsed in a heap. She was not responding to him. His heart sank.

Mrs Knight gently touched Dante's arm. "The ambulance has arrived. I'll be available at your earliest convenience. All the best with your wife and family."

Overcome with emotion, Dante nodded his gratitude to the headmistress. He had no words.

Dante felt confused; his mind raced as he held Alexis's hand throughout the journey and reassured her of his love and unwavering support. Tears ran down his cheeks as he observed the limpness of her body while paramedics checked her vitals. By the time they reached the hospital, she appeared rested and calm. The reassuring nod of the paramedics was very consoling.

After some hours, a doctor approached Dante where he was waiting. "We'll have to keep your wife for few days. She's had a mild heart attack. She's not to receive visitors for a good while yet. Go home and have some rest. We'll be in touch."

Dante drove home in a daze. What was it that he'd noticed that morning? Had her tears been a preamble to this emotional meltdown and subsequent heart attack? He decided to fetch Vic and have him spend time with the family while his mother was in hospital.

If only Alexis knew the high regard that Mr Thadavanal has for our son. Imagine a headmaster giving his student a fortnight, if necessary, to be with his mother. He is known as a brilliant scholar. As parents we've fussed around Tara all the time, but look what a gem Vic is. I'll have to inform Alexis's family about her being in hospital. I hope this will help her parents to relent.

"Dad," Tara said animatedly when Cass opened the door to her father. "Mrs Herbert asked me to design the cover for the creative dancing concert – want to see?"

"*Definitely*, but before you do, say hello to someone who's come all the way to spend the week with you." He smiled as Vic struck a funny pose, causing his sister to shriek with delight.

Cass caught them on camera as they hugged each other excitedly after Vic's performance.

After supper, Bianca allowed the twins to take over her job in the kitchen, stacking the dishwasher and tidying up the kitchen. She returned to the lounge with their dad and Cass, where they enjoyed freshly brewed coffee while they engaged in a private conversation.

"What's happened to Mum, Tara?" Vic asked when they were alone.

"Not sure, Vic, but I'm glad for this break. She's nerve-racking."

"Tara, take it back!" He faced her squarely and placed his hands firmly on her shoulders.

"Come along, kids!" their dad called just then. "Time to go!"

"*Kids?*" they said in unison.

Vic announced theatrically, "It's *Tara* and *Vic, Mr Campbell* – have you got that?"

CHAPTER 36

What a Saturday! Dante put the chores on hold after his mother phoned to tell him that she refused to iron Vic's shirts and trousers.

"They're in such a poor condition, I wouldn't even give them to a charity shop. Your child deserves better, Dante. You and your sisters had to make do with what your dad and I could afford, but even *your* clothes were of a better quality."

Dante was stunned. "Mum, I can't imagine Alexis buying anything inferior. This is unlike—"

"Open your eyes, Dante. Something's not right. Tara gets the best dance costumes that cost the *earth*, yet Vic's uniform is mediocre. Not even children should practise double standards."

Dante was speechless. His mother usually spent hours doing the laundry and mending clothing when necessary. He could not find any logical reason why she would exaggerate. Alexis ordered clothing online and had good taste – though he knew only about Tara – but she would have provided well for their son. He decided to have a word with the headmaster, convinced that someone might have switched clothes in the laundry.

Tara and Vic were always ready to have their namesakes over. Dante agreed to leave them with the couple for the weekend while he took care of Alexis. They were usually good company to have around in a crisis, and the twins loved them.

Vic made a beeline for the grand piano as soon as they arrived and spontaneously played "The Viennese Waltz". Dante danced with Tara, and eventually the elderly couple joined them.

"My, how professional you are," Lady Tamar cooed breathlessly. "Wait till that big birthday comes ... next weekend, isn't it? You're going to be parents of teenagers, Dante. Victor and I will have to do more exercises if we wish to dance throughout the party! We'll have to organize something special for our little stars." She winked at Victor as she fanned her face.

Victor sat in his favourite armchair, chuckling behind a glass of cold water. "Yeah, right, but count me out of these senior-unfriendly dances."

Dante smiled as he stood between the twins. He gave each of them a kiss on the top of the head.

"They're already teenagers, as far as I'm concerned – more like my right and left hand. As long as my scallywags are together, any time with them is a celebration."

Vic bent over and held his stomach mischievously, feigning tummy ache. "I've been having these sharp pains since breakfast. It must be the scrambled eggs that Dad made. I had to take a double portion, because Tara ate very little scrambled eggs. Oooh! The pain is awful ..."

They laughed as Dante playfully chased Vic around the table, waving a balled fist.

Lady Tamar opened her diary. "We haven't discussed the venue for the twins' birthday yet."

Tara spoke in a subdued tone. "Mum said we're not going to invite family. I'll be allowed to invite thirteen friends, and then we'll have a barbecue in the courtyard."

Vic's eyes brimmed with tears. "When Mum phoned me, she told me that I have to stay at the Academy and practise for my music exam. Dad was to bring me cake and presents." Embarrassed, he left the room. Tara followed him, also in tears.

Dante was shaken. He stared unseeing while Lady Tamar followed them, and his mind drifted.

Things are starting to make sense. According to Cass and Bianca, they have spoken to Alexis about her obvious preference for Tara over Vic. They also noticed Tara's aversion to food and her obsession with her weight. How come I missed all this? How do I broach the subject with Tara? How will I convince Vic that his mother loves him, after what he's shared? This is tough. I think I'll ignore what has happened and keep a close eye on Tara's food intake. Broaching the subject might be unwise at this stage. Prudence is key. Why does it hurt so much? I trusted her.

The elderly man touched Dante' arm gently. "You probably prefer being on your own, but I think it's important that you and I talk about this, man to man. Lady Tamar's good with children;

133

she'll manage them just fine. Let me get us a pot of tea – helps de-escalate the struggle to talk freely." He went to prepare a tray for both of them.

Meanwhile, Dante broke down, sobbing loudly with the overwhelming loneliness that he had been feeling for a long time: his wife speaking in riddles, Tara's headmistress sharing about her weight loss and tiredness, Vic being sidelined for his birthday, and his own observations about Alexis's obsession with Tara's dancing.

Dante decided to address these issues without losing his wife's confidence and affecting her health. He so dearly wanted to help his beloved family, but his own helplessness caused him deep pain, anxiety, and anguish. His mind was made up; he knew what he was going to do.

Victor squeezed his shoulder. "You have a friend in me, buddy. Talk about it; it's therapeutic. Get it out of your system, even if it's about your wife. I know you love her dearly, and your winning nature will help her, but you need to be heard too. I'm here for you; please talk to me."

It was a while before Dante could speak. Victor threw him a knowing look.

"I had an experience much earlier … even before we got married. I arranged to meet her parents, and she snapped at me – called off our engagement. It was scary, Victor; I struggled through it. Fortunately, I spoke to my mother, and she created an atmosphere like this: she listened and was very caring, showing great empathy. She helped me to see the bigger picture. It helped me, Victor, but there've been other signs. I was so afraid … embarrassed … scared I'd lose Alexis." He swallowed and looked solemnly ahead of him. "I don't have the heart to speak to my family about my wife. I don't want to lose her."

"You won't lose her, buddy. You would do her a great service if you spoke to her caringly and told her how much you loved her and every member of your family. My wife is a trained psychologist and has a marvellous way with people of all ages – you could not have a more dysfunctional family than mine. Look, I could barely write any of them into my will. We chose Bianca, because of her strong will to overcome her struggles against all odds."

Dante addressed Victor calmly. "But you've also included Cass and Alexis. They're not family."

"They're not family, but they've supported each other far

more than their families have. I know all about Alexis. Bianca told me about it when we visited her at boarding school."

"Wait a minute! What are you telling me? Do you mean you and Bianca are related?"

"No, Bianca was a foundling, but when her mother discovered that her biological parents were African, she placed her in boarding school from a young age and skipped the country. When we discovered how Alexis supported her and a friend, we chose to help all three friends."

Dante was pleasantly surprised to learn how Victor and Lady Tamar had supported Alexis and her friends and was appreciative of how much they had come to love Alexis. He felt reassured that Victor would honour the confidentiality of his story, so he proceeded to open up about his struggles with his wife and her divisiveness towards their children.

"This must be so hard, Dante. I can't imagine having to be a good husband, father, brother, and son with all the drama in your life. No wonder you're overwhelmed and feeling down in the mouth."

"I love my wife, Victor, but as adults we need to rear our children with clearer vision. They're not responsible for what she's been through. She appears to be rejecting Vic – I was horrified at what his headmaster told me recently. Apparently, Alexis had not catered for Vic's basic needs in school. His uniforms were so discoloured that my mother was unable to launder them. Vic made excuses and lied about his mother being ill months ago. The headmaster believed him. I will be taking charge in future. I've made up my mind to assist Alexis with the children. From now on, I want to be included in all aspects of their upbringing: clothing, relationships, education, school information – everything. I've left most of these for Alexis to sort out. It's time I got myself more involved in matters."

"That's brilliant. I'm sure you realize also that Alexis has no ill will," Victor assured him. "But she's probably projecting onto the children what she feels towards her parents. Brigido disowned her when she reclaimed her identity as a teenager. Michaela stood by Brigido and overlooked their daughter's needs. Alexis needs support – at least your children have one parent who's better able to handle this struggle – but we need to find help for her. She has a heart of gold, but she needs emotional support. She needs our understanding of her."

"She's in counselling currently and refuses to see Vic, but she insists that I bring Tara on my next visit. I cannot support that, Victor."

"Use your initiative, and do something creative, Dante." He poured their tea. "Eventually she will see him. Give her time. Empathy is about seeing things from another's point of view. You need not approve, but be there for her. Follow your heart, and make sure Vic is assured of *your* love."

Dante nodded knowingly and sipped his tea. "Victor, do you think it would be wise for me to take the twins to see their grandparents?"

"That's your call, my man. I cannot advise you on that matter, given the experience you already had before your marriage. However, never do things behind your wife's back – there's no blessing on that. Patience and prudence are crucial. I'm with you in this, remember?"

Victor and Dante sat in silence for a long time – each engrossed in his own thoughts. Eventually, after several cups of tea, Victor got up, stretched himself, and broke the silence. "Dante, even if you paid thousands for therapy, unless there's a soft place for Alexis to land in your home, counselling will be futile, because of her deep emotional scars. She needs your non-judgemental support. Make constant efforts as a husband and father to include both your children. Be an agent of change, without waiting for her to alter her behaviour. She's emotionally limited at this stage, and she needs to learn different behaviour patterns. Teach, don't preach! Your own example will speak much louder than your condemnation of her. You married her *for better or for worse*, *in sickness and in health, for richer or poorer.* You have the wealth; the rest will take a lifetime of working at. Work at being patient and prudent."

Dante rose and embraced the elderly man. "Thanks, Victor, I realize that. It's time I listened to her – really listened. I also need to be there for the twins."

"They're two people, Dante," Victor said and smiled. "Start referring to them as individuals and not as 'the twins'. You've done a marvellous job already, both of you. They're great kids!"

CHAPTER 37

L ady Tamar was enjoying hot chocolate with the children – both of whom were in pyjamas – while engaged in an animated conversation. It was clear that their age difference did not matter. Dante smiled when he heard their laughter down the hall, and he decided to join them.

"So, my darlings, Aunty Tamar and Uncle Victor want to host a celebration for your birthday, right here, next Saturday. I know the actual day is Sunday, but I don't think your friends will be available what with going to church and all," Dante said as he sat down with them.

"What if Mum comes and asks what I'm doing home?" Vic asked as he dunked a biscuit.

"Listen, Vic," Dante said as he crouched in front of him. "Your mum has been through a rough time, and when you're a little older, she might be able to talk it over with you. For now, Uncle Victor and Aunt Tamar will be helping the three of us until Mum gets better. You need to trust me on this, all right?" A message bleeped on his mobile, and Dante left the room.

Tara raised her voice. "I don't think it's fair that we support Mum. She told me one thing about our birthday and my brother another. She is clearly in the wrong."

Lady Tamar was very gentle. "Not if you know the full story, honey. When you eventually meet your maternal grandparents, you will love and appreciate your mum much more."

"I think Mum hates her mum and expects us to do the same. How can she expect us to love her if she hates *her* mum?"

Vic went over to his sister. "Tara, Dad's just said we don't know the whole story. Maybe we could ask Mum someday. Dad's right; we need to understand Mum's side. Nan told me, 'People who are hurting hurt others.' So let's just chill and practise for the show at our birthday party."

"I guess so," she said calmly. "But I still want to quit dancing."

Lady Tamar was stunned. *So this is the crux of the matter.* "Quit dancing? Whatever for, Tara?"

Tara's voice quivered. "I want to quit dancing and do *art. Mum* likes dancing, but *I* prefer art. I've tried telling Mum several times, but … she says art's for mediocre students and—"

Vic spoke gently. "You're not mediocre, Tara. You're smart, and it's great that you're doing dancing, but when you start high school, you could change over and do art."

The older woman looked from one to the other. "You're both very talented children, with many opportunities ahead of you. Whatever your parents have decided for you will do you good. When you're older, and the time comes for you to make your own choices, you will know what you've given up."

"I chose music, Aunty Tamar, and Dad allowed me to learn more. I can't think of anything else I'd like better – maybe more instruments." He winked mischievously at Lady Tamar.

Tara sounded bitter. "That's because you're the smart one … the genius in the family. You have peace at boarding school … while I … I have Mom breathing down my neck all day … every day. D'you … do you know that I … I have … have breakfast with Julie next door, because I can't stand her following me all day, every day?"

Lady Tamar was taken aback. "Tara, that sounds quite tough, my angel. Do you want to say some more about it? You know, we've all been hurt in our families, but talking about it somehow helps."

Vic interrupted and spoke in a casual tone. "I only knew the piano when I left home, but I *decided* to play the violin, the viola, and the cello. I did not ask Mum or Dad's permission. I played music because I enjoyed it. If you hate dancing, why don't you drop it and do art? You can always speak to the headmistress and ask to do art in the second term. I would if I were you. I think you're a great artist. You will remember your dance steps, but art's your gift – isn't it so, Aunt Tamar?"

"You're quite right, Vic." Lady Tamar realized how assertive Vic was in comparison to his sister. With minimal support from his mother, he seemed to have developed an emotional robustness well beyond his years. No wonder his headmaster allowed him time out of school to be with his mother. *This boy is a genius intellectually,* and *he's emotionally solid*, she thought.

"That sounds nice," Tara managed to say. "But Mum's paid so much money on costumes – she'll go ballistic." She became quiet, unable to hold back her tears.

Having finished his phone call, Dante came in to greet them before returning home. He touched Tara's cheek tenderly when he saw her tears, and he watched how Vic held her hand.

"Your mum will be home soon; she's on the mend. Lady Tamar, please take care of my scallywags. I'll see you soon." He embraced the children on either side of him and winked an eye at the elderly woman.

The wisdom of Lady Tamar and Lord Victor certainly helped Tara and Vic to grow in empathy towards their mother. Their mother's preference of one sibling over the other made no difference to their own relationship. The way forward was for them to understand that there was a deeper underlying problem that did not involve them at all. This awareness gave the children fresh hope and inner strength.

Dante was proud of his children, very proud indeed!

CHAPTER 38

Dante had an unsettled night, tossing and turning in his bed until morning. He recalled his pain at finding out the night before that Vic had been spending his holidays and mid-term breaks with Lord Victor and Lady Tamar instead of coming home. The fact that this revelation had been made during Vic's speech at the elderly couple's golden wedding celebration shattered him.

Not wanting to disturb Alexis, who was still asleep, Dante picked up his journal – a helpful outlet for his frustrations and anger. It had been suggested by Lord Victor as a monitor for recording his self-talk.

Dante started writing in his journal while waiting for the kettle; hot chocolate always helped him to get back to sleep.

> *Thanks, Victor, for your earlier advice about journaling – at present it's my best option. Your suggestion that I practise patience and prudence in our marriage is working very well. Though I'm not sure how I was expected to accept the information about Vic in the presence of friends and family last night.*
>
> *Initially, I remember feeling absolutely gutted that Vic had chosen to remain at the Academy. I'd thought that it was because of the intensity of his music practice program. He lied by omission – I know he's no longer a kid – but whatever for? If this is his final year, what will happen once he's graduated?*
>
> *I love Alexis, but I can't understand how she's remained unfazed by his disclosure at the*

celebration. Why can't I brush aside the fact that our son chose Lady Tamar and Lord Victor's home over ours? Have we been so unapproachable or too busy with our affairs at school to notice this?

Surely Vic knows that we love him? Last night Alexis appeared nonchalant, barely batting an eyelid when the guests applauded, so what's the point of discussing the matter with her? And Tara must have known about this arrangement; has she deliberately kept it from us? What's going on in this family?

Dante gazed out the kitchen window as dawn was breaking and watched the sunrise lighting the skies. He let his tears roll freely as he painfully acknowledged that his dream of family life was slipping away. Deep sadness filled his heart, and he allowed his tears to flow. He felt utterly alone, abandoned, let down, lonely, and in need of a listening ear.

———✿———

"Morning, Dad." Tara looked bleary-eyed as she entered the kitchen. "Had a good sleep? Hot coffee first thing in the morning usually keeps me alert for the day. Oh good, there's enough water. Bet you've had a warm drink too. We've that in common, Dad," she said with a smile, "taking caffeine to wake us."

The kitchen became silent, apart from the sound of the kettle and the ticking of the clock. Tara smiled as she held her father's hand from her chair opposite his. "What's up, Dad? Cat caught your tongue?"

Dante returned her smile. "Tara, why didn't you tell us that Vic spent his vacations with Aunt Tamar and Uncle Victor? It would have been great having him home with us, don't you think? Was it more convenient for him there than at home with us?"

Tara's heart ached whenever her dad's deep, dark eyes betrayed his inner yearning, but this morning she noticed a certain glow in his eyes despite his questions. Although she and her brother had pledged to remain loyal to each other when one of them was absent, she felt torn. Her dad had been an empowering presence in her life and had taught her the value of character-building opportunities.

"I'd speak to *him* if I were you, Dad," she said eventually, and she noticed her father's eyes shining when she spoke. "Vic will confide in you someday," she said and smiled at him again as she touched his shoulder and took her mug of coffee upstairs.

Dante chose his favourite chair in the walled terrace, leaned back, and stretched out his legs. "Thank you, God, for blessing me with two beautiful children, who have so much to teach me about life. Without my dear wife, Alexis, that would not have been possible. With you in my life, there's nothing that can't be fixed."

He spent his morning pouring out his sentiments to his trusted friend – his journal.

Vic was relieved that he had finally secured a teaching post in the local school, where the majority of the people lived in abject poverty. However, many of the children, especially boys, flunked, ignored school rules, roamed the streets aimlessly, and subsequently landed in trouble with the law.

His dream was to create an alternative lifestyle for boys by providing opportunities for them to acquire music skills according to their range of interests and abilities. This entailed auditioning for a school choir and training with various instruments for a specialized music department. He decided to meet with the parent body to share his dream.

"It will be different from a regular school," Vic said in his address to parents in the community centre. "We need to turn this community around by introducing boys to music – instrumental music – with our own boys' choir and an orchestra. I need your collaboration to uplift this community by changing mindsets and encouraging our children to think beyond their circumstances. We all have something to offer the world, we just need someone to believe in us so that the flame of giving can be ignited and passed on. I'm holding that baton!"

"Excuse me, Mr Campbell," one mother said impatiently. "My husband changes the channel on TV when any orchestra plays. Isn't this a bit old-fashioned for youngsters? They like jazzy music."

Judging by the loud applause and raucous laughter in the room, many people agreed with the speaker as they stood around her with folded arms, nodding as she repeated her point over and over.

Vic made another attempt. "I think it will be different when your sons are part of the orchestra. Why don't you give them a chance? See which parents will change the channel when their sons are part of the concert."

A question arose from the back of the room. "What about the expenses involved? We can't afford fees in the *reg'lar* schools – how will we pay for this *special* school?"

Vic walked towards the back of the room. "That's very practical. What I need is your cooperation," he said. "I'm prepared to do the spadework for this project, but I'll need your support, your willingness to collaborate, and your word that you'll do your share by allowing your sons to practise for an hour every day. I need you to back them – big time!"

"Fair enough," one man answered, and more applause followed. "Can we take a vote on this and give this young man our pledge that we'll stand by him?"

The vote was unanimous. Vic had the parents sign his petition, and together with his covering letter, hand-delivered it to the Education Department – feeling very hopeful and confident.

After countless negotiations with the Education Department, they agreed to subsidize a Boys' Academy of Music. The circuit manager instructed Vic to work in collaboration with the headmaster of a prestigious school during his two-year probationary period. Vic felt pleased about the decision and looked forward to meeting his mentor. He discussed his new venture with Lady Tamar, who offered to assist in his office and attend meetings with him until he could find a suitable receptionist and secretary.

Vic's office was inundated with correspondence, phone calls, and offers for sponsorship. Among his emails was a formal letter from the Education Department requesting that he act as administrator for two years. Thinking that his sister was pulling his leg, he stared at the computer screen as she emphatically reread the contents of the letter. They embraced excitedly as it dawned on them what the message was all about: Vic was in charge of his new project!

This was a godsend to the community, and in no time parents flocked to the school, hoping to find places for their sons and grandsons.

CHAPTER 39

D ante felt honoured to be approached by the Education Department and expressed his willingness to assist a college graduate with his project for the community. He discussed with the school board the possibility of adopting this school by making a substantial annual donation.

The rationale for starting such a project for boys was particularly heart-warming, because his and Alexis's project had taken shape twenty-five years ago, and the dropout rate among girls in the area had been remarkably low ever since. Thankfully someone was now looking out for the boys. He longed to meet this young person to affirm him or her for this wonderful initiative.

The door opened, and Vic, looking dapper in his dark suit, and Tara, with a white blouse tucked into her dark pencil skirt, made a deep impression on the board members as they entered the conference hall. There was a stunned silence in the room until the friendly couple reached out to greet everyone formally yet professionally. An electric shock seemed to pass through his body when Vic made eye contact with his mentors: Dante and Alexis.

Dante was appreciative of the serendipity that was occurring within his family. What a privilege to be working in partnership with Vic, who was to direct a new project similar to that which he and Alexis had started more than twenty-five years ago! Ironically, Alexis, after obtaining her licentiate, had pursued disadvantaged girls who were musically inclined and needlessly dropped out of school. Alexis smiled warmly now at Dante and Tara.

A departmental representative rose to her feet and addressed the board members: "Ladies and gentlemen, I was asked to read a formal letter on behalf of the Education Department. I have copies for each of you – if you'd care to open your blue files. I have highlighted the part that pertains to my role here, and then I will leave you to continue." She read the paragraph:

> As the circuit manager of schools in this county, I have undertaken to appoint Mr Dante Campbell as supervisor to the Boys' Academy for the next two years. Mr Victor Campbell is to be the administrator of the aforementioned school. His appointment will run concurrently with that of the supervisor. Mr Campbell (senior) will scrutinize all pro formas of application forms, letters of acceptance, banking details of sponsors, and will oversee the enrolment of students aged twelve to eighteen. A quarterly report covering these important aspects is expected.

A tumultuous applause followed as members of the board rose to congratulate Dante and Victor. Alexis smiled demurely and joined her husband in first shaking their son's hand and then embraced her daughter warmly. The Campbells agreed to meet in their family home to discuss the ramifications of the entire letter, followed by a meeting with the board of trustees.

Tara helped Benita with the grocery-shopping list, while her parents and brother went ahead to the walled terrace to engage in discussions about Vic's new project. She was tasked with the minute-taking for the time being.

"Dad, Mum, I had no idea that our school project was to be launched under your supervision and that we'd be temporarily affiliated to your leadership," Vic began. "I know you're highly trusted and have a high ranking at the Education Department, but this was not what we envisaged when we applied for a school subsidy."

"Son, there's no need to explain," Dante said. "Things happen for a purpose, and our learning will be mutual. Fact is, history's repeating itself. Your mum did the same years ago."

Vic continued. "I'll be moving into my own apartment soon, so we won't have to collide at home and at school. Tara will be coming with me. I made my decision even before I knew you'd be in charge, Dad, but now I'm even more convinced that I'm doing the right thing."

"Just like that?" Alexis asked. "Are you asking or informing us?"

"Informing you," Vic said. "I think it's fair, now that I'll be earning my own salary. It's important for me to think and work independently. At school I will surely welcome your input and critique." He winked at his father and smiled mischievously.

"I was referring to Tara," Alexis said, her eyes flaring. "Have you been brainwashing her again, like you did with the dancing? You were always a bad influence on her. I knew you were up to something when you tried to embarrass us about staying with Lady Tamar and Lord Victor during your holidays. I should have insisted that we call you *Brigido*. You're just like him."

Tara walked in on their conversation and blinked hard, her hand to her mouth. There was no way that she was going to remain silent and watch her brother being sideswiped. He deserved much more for being the gentleman he had become against all odds. She addressed her mother in an even tone, allowing her tears to flow unchecked.

"Mum, if anyone's brainwashed me, it definitely wasn't Vic. He encouraged me to follow my heart when we were mere teenagers, and I did. Isn't it time we made amends as a family, instead of blaming, accusing, and fault-finding? My brother has matured in the face of so much adversity. What support have *you* given Vic? And look how he's coped all the years. He's come out much stronger than me, and today he's a music mogul in the making."

Dante, more composed at this stage, contemplated what Vic and Tara had just disclosed. He felt saddened by Alexis's reactions to them, especially to Vic, who remained respectful towards his mother irrespective of her obvious disregard for him for so many years.

"Alexis, I think you and I need to talk," Dante said. "Let's finish this conversation later, shall we?" He turned to their children. "How about the two of you organizing supper? We'll catch up with you in a bit. I think your mother and I need to sort out a few things."

"Sounds good," Vic said, kissing his mother on her cheek and gently touching his father's arm.

Tara acknowledged both her parents and left the room, walking arm in arm with her brother as they headed towards the garden for a long walk.

———————❀———————

Tara and Vic served the starter of poached salmon with quick Caesar salad, followed by the main meal: king prawn, chorizo, and new potatoes.

Alexis was clearly uncomfortable, but Dante made every effort to draw her into the conversation.

Tara initiated the discussion by showing pictures of the apartment that she and Vic were to share. "They're basically two flats side by side – it's the one Dad rented before you two moved here. Aunty Bianca and Aunty Cass were very excited, but they said they didn't want to disclose anything. They told us to tell you about this venue before we moved in."

Alexis smiled broadly at Dante. "Is there anything you wish to say about that, Dante?"

Blushing to the roots of his hair, Dante said. "I first cast eyes on your mother when she joined our staff. I was smitten, so I used to follow her in my car till I discovered where she lived. When her apartment was up for sale, I was more interested in knowing where your mum lived than I was in the flat. Eventually I earned both her confidence and the apartment."

"Oh wow!" Vic said. "Then, Mum, this was your choice that we unknowingly chose."

Dante was touched. "Vic, you and your mother have so much in common. Even this 'Oh wow' that you constantly exclaim. She has not used it since we got married. Seems you've taken it over. You also have her music talent, her business acumen, and now you've chosen the very apartment she chose before we met."

"Aunty Verushka said the same thing. She said I have Mum's gift for drawing out the best in people. I think it's because of the number of fellow students whom I helped with mathematics, accounting, and physics. I used to help students over weekends and during the holidays, but we inadvertently overlooked the time, and the chef took a stand by not allowing the guys to keep our food. Aunt Tamar used to invite us for meals, and this took care of our problem."

Alexis spoke in a miraculously quiet voice. "Your father's right. You *do* take after me in many ways: Aunty Bianca and Aunty Cass were students with me at school, and I used to assist them with their studies. They did not have the support of their families. I also chose music without any encouragement from my parents. I still have very strong willpower."

147

Dante touched her arm affectionately. "That's what I loved about you from the time you stepped into our school. I knew from the day I met you that we were going to be together for life. I am so proud of you today for sharing that information with Vic and Tara."

"That's so touching, I'm drowning in my tears," Tara said. "Dad always said Vic takes after you, Mum, but you thought I was the one. What made you want me to dance, Mum?"

Tara walked over, sat closer to her mother, and gently placed her head against her mum's shoulder. In that tender moment between them, it seemed as though Alexis made an about-turn. She made eye contact with Vic and Tara and allowed them to see her tears and hear about her struggles. Her features appeared softer, and when Vic came over to sit opposite his sister, she allowed her son to dab her cheeks as the tears streamed endlessly down her face.

"It was something I always longed to do – more out of revenge, because my parents did not like me dancing. One day I'll tell you more. I wanted to prove how graceful and becoming dancing could be. It was not meant to be a punishment, Tara; I hope you understand that."

"Of course not, Mum. All the signs of your love were there, but I was not enjoying it too much.

"I used to confide in Julie, but she always told me how good I was at it. I often cried in my bed and slept very little. I found it hard to eat, because I was mildly depressed, I think. When you became sick, I made desperate attempts to regain my eating habits. I'm just grateful that you and Dad never scolded or accused me of being anorexic. It was not an eating disorder; it was my attempt to get out of dancing. The more time I spent with you, the more you seemed to pressure me about dancing. I wanted to break away from dancing, but I did not know how."

"I am so sorry, my girl, it was not about you at all," Alexis said. Then, touching Vic's cheek with the back of her hand, she said. "And Vic, you have your dad's temperament – placid and forgiving. I am so sorry for what I've put you through, my son. My son ..." She swallowed her emotions. "I'm so proud of you as my son. You've turned out to be such a gentleman in spite of all I've put you through. I promise to make it up to you. Both of you deserve more."

Vic gently touched his mother's hand. "Mum, I knew there was some suffering in your life. Nan told me that people hurt others when they're hurting, and from that day I started asking God to help you and me. It was easy for me to play my music, because I knew you wouldn't pressure me into doing anything else. I was very young when I discovered my love for music. I also knew about Tara's artistic ability. I did not mean to defy you, Mum, but I encouraged Tara to change over because I knew she'd make you proud one day – and she has. You should see her portfolio!"

Dante was amazed at this miracle unfolding before his eyes: Alexis. For the first time in years, the woman he had fallen in love with was emerging like a butterfly from a cocoon within a matter of hours. This was his dream come true, and he was delighted. He found himself loving his wife and family more in their vulnerability, as each one disclosed deep feelings and allowed the others to express theirs. Vic's forgiving heart and Tara's wisdom touched him deeply.

CHAPTER 40

lexis smiled as she read an invitation from the local parish priest, Fr Martin, who requested assistance with a new parish choir. He suggested that Alexis audition the youth and thereby ignite the embers of the parish's music ministry. She wondered whether she should agree to this or ignore it. Wordlessly she showed the invitation to Dante, and he shared her excitement.

Why not? Dante mused. *This should be an excellent route to audition for our music academy. Surely Vic could assist us? He knows the most up-to-date methods of auditioning, and he might find some candidates for his department. I'd love to hear what he has to say.*

Dante rubbed his hands ecstatically and suggested that they pop into Vic's office with the news. "Come along, son – we've something to show you."

Vic read the invitation and smiled at his parents. "On condition that we consider this as a family project. The church choir has far more ramifications than a school does," he said. "You and Mum have more experience; I'm au fait with the instruments. Mum, you have an exceptional ear for music – you'd be great! And as far as I can remember, Dad" – he chuckled – "you've sung every day of your life. I remember the songs by the Beatles that you used to sing to Tara and me. Fact is, you always sang, even when we worked in the garden or when you pottered around in the garage."

Dante was highly amused. "I was so desperate to get the two of you to sleep then – I more than likely hypnotized you in my desperation to get some work done. I agree with the idea of a family project. Sounds like fun to me."

"Vic," Alexis said, "this is also a great opportunity for you to get more involved outside your school. Once you've completed your PhD studies, this exposure will come in very handy for your CV and subsequent promotion. That does not trivialize your outreach to the parish, but you'll need all the experience you can muster to build up confidence in your music career."

"That sounds great, Mum. How about us sharing the task of auditioning and asking Tara to do the art displays for advertising? That way she'd also be helped to build up her art career."

"Oh wow!" Tara said as she walked in on their conversation. "What an excellent way of giving back to the community, especially the parish. We won't have to smile and drive past Fr Martin anymore," she said. "This might be our opportunity to meet him and become part of the parish life. We've been kind of lapsed – some of us were rather *col-lapsed*." She nodded mischievously at her mother, and everyone laughed.

Having communicated their response to the community, Alexis and her family set the wheels in motion for the auditioning to be held in their family home. Dante and Alexis agreed to audition sopranos, mezzo-sopranos, and alto voices, while Vic assessed the children's abilities at the piano, violin, viola, and cello. Tara was happy to take photos and display them in the community hall for the perusal and appreciation of the children, their parents, teachers, and peers.

By the end of the mid-term break, the parish had earned a new family to the congregation who also headed a very promising choir and a new orchestral group.

Fr Martin was thrilled with the assurance of sponsorship from local supermarkets, a Swiss company and, of course, the family's guardian angels, Lady Tamar and Lord Victor.

CHAPTER 41

lexis expected Lady Tamar to call, so when she went to answer the front doorbell, she shrieked with delight at seeing Dante there with an armful of red roses. Meanwhile, Tara and Vic seemed to appear from nowhere, singing "Happy Birthday" to her.

"Mum," Tara eventually said. "You look awesome – like you're ready for the Oscars. Talk about power dressing! I've got to take a picture; please stand next to Dad. Come along, we can't be late!"

"Don't tell me this is another set-up, Tara!" Alexis said. "You and your dad are so alike – rascals to the hilt."

"You're spot on," Tara said with a giggle. "But you and Vic are ridiculously gullible – look how I got both of you to dress up for the occasion!"

There was a buzz of eager anticipation amongst Dante and the children as they made their way through the long country roads. Alexis, while casually opening and then closing the glove compartment, caught an address on the satnav. She recognized it immediately and sat up a little straighter, frozen in annoyance.

Recalling the caring words of her counsellor, Revocate, was helpful: "Anger is a secondary emotion. There's another feeling beneath it; listen to that one before you lash out. Remember: they're *your* feelings; nobody causes them. They are earlier feelings that are triggered because they need to be dealt with, so choose your responses wisely. You're in charge of your life."

Alexis gazed into the distance, took a deep breath, and calmly said, "Dante, please stop at the supermarket. I'd like to buy one or two things, but you'll need to bring your wallet."

A smile played around Dante's lips as he recalled buying her birthday roses at that very shop; he hoped she'd miss that aisle.

Alexis took encouragement from his smile and prayed that she could have just five minutes of privacy with him. Since her cardiac arrest, it had been recommended that she deal with her repressed emotions. Revocate was the best therapist anyone could have. Deep-breathing exercises in the midst of anger certainly helped calm her down whilst she remained in touch with her feelings.

The supermarket was jam-packed with its regular customers when Alexis addressed Dante.

"Dante, according to the satnav, we're heading for my family home. I've forgiven my parents and siblings – you know that – but I cannot walk into their lives unannounced. They have their own journey to make. It'd be grossly unfair to put Vic and Tara through possible humiliation."

"Alexis, as a family, we can no longer allow you to live on the periphery. You deserve better –and have been through enough. Remember our discussion about transformation being a personal journey from the inside out? This is part of that journey – and we're in this together."

Her cheeks were glowing pink with shy pleasure as she enveloped Dante in a warm embrace. "I can't tell you how much this means to me."

Cathy and Zoë met them at the front door before Alexis reached for the doorbell. They said nothing – at least not with words. But the embrace among the three sisters spoke volumes as they stood holding each other for quite a while before drawing apart and wiping their tears.

"Alexis, it's about time," Maria said as she walked in on them. She too gave her a hug. "Now that we've all arrived, please listen up: We'd like you to get to know each other by meeting in the various rooms of this house. Each door has a distinct name on the door. Husbands, you'll be meeting in the Red Room – she pointed in the direction of the rooms. "Cousins, you're in the Blue Room, and we sisters are in the Yellow Room.

"Our agendas are posted on notice boards inside. Drinks and canapés are waiting – we'll meet at two o'clock in the Pearl Room, which is the main room. Ciao!"

Alexis bristled visibly. Just hearing these instructions came as a reminder of her childhood and brought memories flooding back.

Suddenly she felt a single tear flow all the way down her cheek. She scanned the house for her parents, but there was no sign.

Marcia was already in the Yellow Room, and when she saw Alexis, she opened her arms to welcome her. Ancilla and Terése moved towards Alexis, and she took a hand of each and allowed them to lead her to a sumptuously decorated room with high-backed wing chairs arranged in a semicircle. Maria, Cathy, and Zoë followed, and as if on cue, the girls spontaneously held hands and allowed their tears to speak for them.

Over the next hour or so, the girls caught up with news about themselves and their families. Marcia waited for a lull, and then she rose and addressed her sisters.

"Girls," Marcia smiled through her tears. "Words are inadequate to express how happy I am that we're all together today. It was Vic and Tara who initiated this meeting as a gift to you, Alexis, and they couldn't have chosen a better day than today. Someone else has asked me to read this letter on your birthday, so your visit nicely coincides with both requests. Please bear with me and ignore my tears." Marcia removed a letter from its envelope and read:

> My dear Marcia, Maria, Ancilla, Terése, Cathy, Zoë, and Alexandra,
>
> Your father and I have decided to downsize by moving into a smaller complex in Karbo Estate, just outside London. It is cosy and convenient, with much less time spent on cleaning and cooking, as these are being catered for by the staff that head this project. In this way we have more time to relax and enjoy each other's company.
>
> We have refurbished the house by using the three primary colours to mark what was once your bedrooms and living quarters. The main room, the Pearl Room, is where we gathered as a family, the main bedroom and kitchen.
>
> The house was originally meant to become the property of our son – as part of the Versini legacy – but because we have no sons and only one grandson, your father and I have decided to entrust the entire property into the hands of Alexandra and her family.

Alexandra, I long to see you and make up to you, but your father has disallowed this and threatened to annul our marriage should I make any attempt to betray him. It's been thirty years since I've had a conversation with you, and that's the reason why the very room you're in is called the Pearl Room. You are my pearl, honey, because you were like the grain of sand lodged in our home with the layers of nacre that have helped you to become the precious woman that you are today.

Please forgive me for my blindness and pray that I too, like you, may become a woman of courage – one who stands by her convictions without depending on others for approval. I'd love to meet with you – not alone. I want your father with me. This has been my prayer for many years, and I've continued to live in the hope that we would meet again as parents with our daughter, Alexis, the name you've requested as your preferred name.

I love you, Alexis; I love you with all my heart. Please forgive me for having wronged you by not claiming my place as the heart of the home. May your relationships with your sisters grow ever stronger as you allow the millions of microscopic molecules of goodness amongst you to align for the light of God to pass through. My hope is that your children will appreciate the rich tapestry of love, joy, and peace that has remained the glue of your relationships, irrespective of our bad parenting over the years.

You, my dear daughters, have strong qualities of loyalty, integrity, and authentic love. I am proud of you. Somehow I seem to have lost my foothold in the mire of cowardice and pride, with the mistaken idea that I was being loyal and supportive. I love your father very much, and I respect his principles, but I refuse to allow myself to be drawn any further into a trap that separates me from my beloved seven daughters.

Every day my desire deepens – that we be
united as a loving family, with Dad beside me.
Lovingly,
Mum
XXXXXXX

Each of the sisters was visibly touched by their mother's endearing letter and quietly wiped away her tears. None of them wanted to comment on the contents of the letter, but when they each received a personal copy in its own envelope, they spontaneously rose and formed a circle with their arms around each other's waists.

They all sat down, except Marcia, who looked ponderously at each of them in turn, her gaze finally resting on her youngest sister.

"You seem fine, Alexis, but how are you *really* coping? Please don't airbrush your feelings. Dr Phil says, "You can't fix what you don't own." I heard something like that on one of his shows. I know Dad has so much owning up to do; I'm not sure when he'll get fixed. Does that bother you?"

Inwardly Alexis shuddered as she recalled her weak physical condition of years ago. She patted a chair beside her for Marcia before she spoke.

"I developed a heart condition when my children were teenagers, and I put it down to my anger and resentment. The doctor recommended that someone accompany me as I dealt with my repressed emotions. You can imagine what that was like. My poor children – I was no better than Dad when I showed preference for one child over the other."

"That must have been quite hard for you, Alexis," Maria said as she drew her chair closer. "You were always very sensitive to people's feelings. What happened?"

"There was something that Oprah said that became a changing moment in my life," Alexis said, taking out her purse to retrieve her notebook. "She said, 'Forgiveness is giving up the hope that the past will change.' I bawled my eyes out when I first heard this, but once I embraced it, it was as though the world had opened its doors to me."

"That's big, Alexis," Marcia said as she placed her precious letter in her handbag. "You've always been very wise. I think that's what suffering does to us; it changes our perceptions about life. I dreaded meeting you, Alexis," she added. "Mum prepared us, though we didn't know the details until tonight. I was afraid of what you might say, leaving us feeling totally helpless."

"Yeah, me too," Maria said. "For years, it seemed that not even prayers worked, that nothing would change our parents. It took a while for me to understand and accept the fact that I cannot change anyone but me. 'How silly,' I thought, but with time, I saw the sense of it."

"You've always been part of our lives too," Alexis said. "Our family conversations and stories to our children always included you. They've always known about you, but I've never disclosed the details."

"Yeah," Marcia said, "that was a promise we made among ourselves – that our children would not lose their connection with their aunt and grandparents. By the way, it's gone two o'clock," she announced. "Let's see whether our menfolk and the cousins have bonded while they were working."

"Working? What do you mean?" Alexis asked, following Marcia through each section of the house.

They found the men enjoying themselves while preparing the family cookout, unfazed by the request that they get on with the barbecue while their wives settled family business. They added logs to the already blazing fire, grinning and winking at each other as more and more stories emerged about the stock market, cars, cricket, housing, and politics.

"Oh wow, this is brilliant!" Alexis exclaimed. "I thought it was women who liked to talk – look at them, as if they've known each other for years. I wonder what our children are up to."

Alexis gazed around the room and found it interesting that none of her sisters had any sons – Vic was the only nephew among their parents' fifteen grandchildren. His cousins clearly adored him and teased him mercilessly.

Zoë, Cathy, and Ancilla helped to carry dishes to the dining room, full of smiles as they enjoyed the easy banter among their husbands and children. Cathy said it reminded her of their teenage years when they'd had loads of good fun, laughter, and teasing among themselves.

The women and their daughters helped to organize tastefully prepared salads, sliced French and garlic loaves, rolls, and roasted bread on tables that were set up in the spacious room

Marcia and Dylan saw that the deliciously barbecued chops, juicy sausages, spuds in foil, chicken drumsticks, and spare ribs in stainless-steel containers were well spaced among the other dishes. Very soon the room was filled with the delicious aroma of food lovingly prepared.

Cathy operated her DVD video camera and walked in and out of rooms, delighted at seeing the family bonding and enjoying their time together. Just before Marcia called everyone to the room, Cathy angled the camera towards the door as they all gathered around the tables.

Vic had organized glasses on a tray for everyone and was responsible for the bar, but he disappeared and had everyone wondering where he had gone. Meanwhile, Dante distributed champagne to everyone and invited the oldest among them to propose a toast to Alexis, the youngest Versini sibling.

Marcia stepped forward and took charge. "Ladies and gentlemen," she announced, "let us begin our celebration in a typically aristocratic fashion. Kindly raise your glasses!" And as they did so, the wall lit up with the lyrics of "A Song for Alexis", by Tara and Vic.

Vic walked in playing the "Happy Birthday" tune on his violin. He and Tara sang the first verse of their composed lyrics, their dad the second, and then everyone joined in singing the rest of the song, which ended with three cheers to Alexis. A tumultuous applause followed, and then everyone took turns in congratulating Alexis on her birthday.

Ancilla and Maria assumed the role of hostesses, as they bustled between the tables making sure that everyone was having a good time.

Vic went around topping up drinks and eventually made his way to stand beside his mother.

"That was such a beautiful song, Vic!" she said. "I've been writing poetry for years, but I didn't know you shared that talent. Thank you for the kind words; they're very special."

"Mum," Vic said enthusiastically, "why don't you let me have a peek at your poems? I'd like to study your style of writing."

"Remind me on your next visit home. No access to the private ones, but I'll share the others with you." She felt her face colouring as she remembered some of the poems she had written to Dante before they were married.

This, she thought, *is an ideal time to make my announcement.* She smiled warmly at Vic as she rose and tinkled a glass for everyone's attention.

"Thank you for this most precious birthday celebration ever. I am deeply indebted to my six beautiful sisters, who graciously dignified Vic and Tara's request to celebrate with the rest of our family. I am so proud to be associated with each of you – my beautiful nieces and handsome brothers-in-law. Thanks for being such a wonderful bunch."

Dante stood beside Alexis and held her hand as he announced that he would be accompanying their children with their favourite song, "Perhaps Love". Vic and Tara stood on either side of their mother as they sang the duet to her.

Everyone was in awe of the unique brother-and-sister relationship that was so well demonstrated in their harmonious voices.

While everyone applauded, Alexis held her son and daughter close and smiled at Dante. Her appreciation of this exceptional celebration was not as great as her gratitude to God for her parents and siblings, from whom she had received her first lessons of love.

CHAPTER 42

Alexis was lying in bed, unable to fall asleep, while she reflected on how much she had experienced since the adversity in her life had started. Tears trickled down the sides of her face as she recalled the memories that had made such a huge impact on her life.

She recalled her years away from her family: the boarding school, the friendships, her teaching career, and the other doors that had opened when her family door had closed behind her. Her beloved nan had also endured the estrangement from her granddad and eventually lost him in death without an opportunity to reconcile. Even this sorrow in her life had not deterred Nan from loving and reaching out to her when she began her new pathway as a fledgling in the teaching profession. Bianca and Cass had been her pillars of support even after she'd met her beloved Dante and they'd begun their own family. Alexis knelt down beside her bed and prayed aloud:

> Dear God, I can hardly believe the struggles I've been through and how my life has turned around because of the patience, care, love, and acceptance of good friends, my husband, and children. You showed yourself as even greater, because though I've made so many mistakes – judged my parents, blamed Nan and my sisters, despised Vic, favoured Tara over her brother, gravitated towards girls and ignored the boys – you never failed me. You even gave me Dante as my greatest gift. Dante helped me to believe in myself and reminded me that

nobody defines who I am. He has been such a gentleman in bringing me back to my children, my family, and you, my God.

Thank you for helping me to grow in self-love, courage, and forgiveness because of, and in spite of, the adversity in my life.

————— ❀ —————

"You want to do what?" Brigido asked Michaela as she sat in the breakfast nook making her to-do list out loud.

"I want to drive to Brighton and meet Lady Tamar and Lord Victor – they're getting on in years, and I feel awful having ignored all their invitations. I'm longing for a get-together with them."

"What stops them from coming here?" Brigido said, looking annoyed. "Is our place not good enough?"

"There's nothing wrong with the place, but I'd rather go out and see them than have them around your unwelcoming face."

"Ouch! That's nasty, Michaela. What's eating you these days?"

"Nothing. I'm just so tired of having to dance to your tune. I've done it for too long and have lost contact with my baby girl for all these years. I've missed her, Brigido, truly I have."

"You cannot bring back her childhood, Michaela; that's ridiculous. Move on – that's what I say."

"That's exactly what I'll be doing over the next week – moving on. I'll be away for a week." But when she saw his face, she said, "Go along and sulk, Brigido. I said I'm going to make amends. Move on I will, Brigido Versini. You'll see! The first train comes within an hour."

Brigido poured himself a cup of tea and wordlessly sat down beside his wife. She seemed to be deep in thought again – a habit she'd developed lately. Maybe she was not feeling too well.

Michaela's eyes brimmed with tears as she remembered that fateful day thirty years ago.

My beautiful child was asking to be reared as our daughter, but I was too absorbed in what Brigido preferred. I considered his heart condition as more important than our daughter's yearning for her identity as a girl. She was polite, gentle, and courageous – so very courageous. I blamed her, insulted her, banished her, ignored her, punished her, deprived her, and rejected her. On the odd occasions when I saw her with her nan, I looked past her. She's the only one who didn't have special birthdays with us. I became a hardened, unforgiving monster.

Brigido's comment brought her back to the reality. "We've given her the house; what more do you want? Are we supposed to walk on our knees to her? Not me, sorry!" He walked out.

Michaela made her way to the Victoria line and studied her notebook for the last lap of her journey. London, Euston, was just four stops away from taking a taxi to her destination. She wondered about the reception she'd get, but then she brushed the thought aside quickly.

Her journal had become her closest ally; she turned the pages and read her recent entry:

> *Michaela, it's no use worrying what anyone will say to or about you; you've been a stubborn fool listening to no one else but Brigido as if you shared a backbone, brain, and common sense.*
>
> *Look what you've put your baby daughter through and how her sisters did your job when she went through her teenage years. She landed in hospital, and you allowed Brigido to talk you out of going to see her. Even animals nurture their young and protect them from predators.*
>
> *At Marcia's wedding you totally ignored her, even though she looked stunning and sang like a bell. She stood alone, because you let Brigido pull you away, and she was left holding on for dear life to her violin, looking so vulnerable, while her sisters paired up with the groomsmen. You saw the lost look on her young face and ignored her when she needed you most. What a shame!*
>
> *You kept quiet when Brigido parked the cars around the corner and told me to write her that note that the cars were due for a service. What were you thinking? Did you check whether she had any money for transport? You had no consideration for her travelling in the pouring rain when you saw she had no protection – not even a jumper. Cathy wept for her sister, as did Marcia, Ancilla, and Terése, but you dismissed them and told them*

to grow up. They have since, but you still have lots of growing up to do.

Over the years, Alexis lost touch with her nan and sisters and befriended students who had worse circumstances than she should have had. She took them into her apartment – which you and Brigido objected to, because her nan helped and gave them a place to call home. Look where they are today. They're dignified, respectful, and highly trusted – all because Alexis saw beyond her own struggle and recognized the pain of three young girls. According to Ancilla, the girls were weak students – one was known to be the school bully – and social outcasts whom Alexis genuinely showed love to by assisting them with difficult subjects and encouraging them to have a study routine. She brought them along when her sisters visited, sharing family life and love with them.

When Marcia invited you recently to celebrate Alexis's birthday and a reunion of the siblings and their families, you cowered like a frightened puppy – too cowardly to put in an appearance. What a golden opportunity you had when Brigido's family legacy matured. You let Marcia present Alexis with the lion's share of our material wealth. She deserves your remorse for the emotional abuse you've put her through – that's what counts more.

You were present when all the girls had their babies – they wanted you there – but what about Alexis?

Dear God, each time I think of how she's been deprived of my love, my heart sinks. I am so sorry, so very sorry. Please help me to do this well. No more easy roads from here. My daughters have taught me so much. They've forgiven me, looked past my faults and failings, been exemplary mothers and wives, and shown devotion to one another. What happened to all my good intentions when I married Brigido Versini?

Bring Brigido out of victim mode and help him to find his way back to our baby daughter and her family. She deserves both of us in her life – and so does her family. Whatever it is that he is still holding onto from his past, let him cast it aside, and make the road ahead of him wider and clearer. Give us the chance to reconcile with our child and give us time with her – enough time.

Michaela leaned back as the taxi wound its way through the attractive beachside suburb. She couldn't imagine Brigido's cousin Victor and his wife living anywhere else.

I used to love Brigido's stories about this village when he was a young lad, she thought. *I wonder what it was that drove them bananas. I'm sure none of them remember what the feud was about. No wonder he's still so resentful and bitter. Whatever feelings Alexis triggered, only God knows – or does he?* She smiled.

The taxi driver's voice interrupted her reverie. "Number 51, madam! Enjoy your visit. Good couple living there – everyone's always welcome. Give them my regards. Tell them old Larry Poppas brought you safely. Goodbye now!"

Lady Tamar looked exquisite as ever in her dark trousers and shimmering floral top. Her face lit up with a beautiful smile as she greeted Michaela in a warm embrace.

"Come inside, my dear," Lady Tamar said warmly. "How lovely to see you again. You're still as young and beautiful as ever." They walked arm in arm along the corridor until they reached Michaela's room.

Michaela felt overwhelmed by the warm welcome and classy suite, and her words were tinged with emotion. "Thank you, Lady Tamar. I don't deserve to be spoilt like this. I've been an awful mother …" She sobbed. "I've missed my baby … my beautiful baby girl. I've hurt her … Lady Tamar, I've hurt my baby. Your kindness … your compassion and care … your love has remained intact. How is it … that I want to love like you? I've wanted to so badly … but I couldn't … Lady Tamar, so many heartaches. I felt so utterly alone … in so much pain. Why did I listen to him, Lady Tamar?"

"Shhh," Lady Tamar soothed. She sat beside Michaela, gently holding her arm and stroking her back. "Maybe you thought you were being a faithful wife. We learnt that from our mothers. At least we have each other for sounding off now. Let out the pain,

Michaela. You'll feel much better afterwards. There's nothing worse than beating ourselves up over the past; it does hurt, I know."

As Lady Tamar opened Michaela's suitcase, and saw the transparent folder containing childhood photos of Alexis, her eyes rose and met Michaela's, and a moment of perfect understanding connected them. Michaela's gentle nod gave Lady Tamar the go-ahead, and she placed the clothes in drawers or on hangers and put the suitcase away.

She sat on the chair beside Michaela. "Is there anything else you wish to say, honey?"

"There's so much that I'm feeling." She sobbed. "I feel wretched, ashamed, and mad at myself."

"That's to be expected, my dear," Lady Tamar said gently. "Allow me to show you another window through all this."

"Please do. I've always been very critical about spirituality and psychology, but at this stage I'm virtually grasping at straws. I need all the support I can get. I want my life back, Lady Tamar."

"Michaela, many years have come and gone, and I can understand all the regrets and good memories that you wish you'd had. I'm with you in that pain. I've always understood that – always. But let me tell you the good news: you must have done something good as parents. Your children have turned out to be well-balanced, sensitive, and caring mothers; loyal; compassionate; and very personable. So much good has come out of this family adversity.

"When Alexis went through rough times, she alienated herself. When their beloved nan was placed in a nursing home, she barely recognized anyone, except Alexis. She was the only one allowed to visit and take care of her nan's personal needs. Alexis became her sole beneficiary, and none of your other daughters begrudged her this. Your daughters are gems – their husbands are blessed, and their children echo their parents' disciplined, caring, and polite conduct."

"That's true," Michaela said. "They have an admirable rapport that's so heart-warming."

"Michaela, the past will continue to linger and keep you stuck in your guilt, shame, and anger. There must have been lots of pain, but let's look at what the present is like and see how you want to move forward."

"I want to let go of the past," Michaela said eventually. "Just having shared that bit and then listened to you seems to have lifted quite a load from my heart. I feel much lighter, with more energy. In fact, I'm hungry – haven't felt so for weeks. You're a great tonic, Lady Tamar!"

"Well, you're just in time for a warm dinner. Megan's made what I recall as your favourite – broccoli tossed in butter with chestnuts, and there are one or two other dishes as well. Come!"

CHAPTER 43

"We've been invited to an orchestral concert tonight," Lady Tamar informed Michaela. "Please wear the cerise dress in your wardrobe. Ken and Owen will be doing your hair and make-up – after you've had your shower. That's in an hour."

"I didn't bring a cerise dress, Lady Tamar; that must be yours or from a previous guest," Michaela said with a frown.

"It's yours now." Lady Tamar nudged her playfully. "It will do you a world of good to go out and enjoy some light fun. We've been invited for a light snack beforehand so that you don't feel hungry during the show.

Michaela was impressed by the excellent recital by the young performers and amazed by their confidence and apparent bond with the conductor. The soloists reminded her of her own daughters; she recalled how often they'd practised before shows.

It brought a fresh flow of tears as she remembered young Alexis's yearning to play an instrument and how her father had insisted that she focus on cricket and baseball. He had insisted, "Music is for the girls."

Michaela felt a gentle touch on her shoulder. There was only one person in her family who had ever done that – Alex! Lady Tamar and Lord Victor stepped back and smiled as they watched another miracle unfold.

Mother and daughter embraced for what seemed an eternity. Michaela wept as she made eye contact with her daughter after thirty years.

"Thanks for coming, Mum!" Alexis said gently as she laid her head on her mother's shoulder. "You've made my day. Let me introduce you to my colleagues."

"Just a minute, honey," Michaela said tearfully; the words seemed stuck in her throat. "I am so sorry. Please forgive me, my girl."

"Michaela," Alexis said playfully. "I moved on ages ago. I have more reasons to rejoice than to be sad. Can you be happy for me from now on, Mum dearest?"

"I already am. Seeing you tonight has lifted a heavy load from my heart. I'd love to spend time with you and your family someday. If you'll welcome me, of course."

"No need to ask, Mum," she said, embracing her. "We'll soon take you up on that offer."

Delighted about the exciting evening, Michaela smiled warmly as she pencilled in her journal:

> *Lady Tamar and Alexis are generations apart, and yet so alike. They've taught me to have a vision by shifting my thinking towards my goals and letting go of the past. Yes! I like that! When I travel home, I shall indeed be a few emotional milligrams lighter. Life is beautiful, and I'm going to show Brigido how worthwhile this journey has been.*

Michaela bid a warm adieu to Lord Victor and Lady Tamar before boarding the taxi for home. There was a spring in her step as she made her way back – she had so much to share with Brigido.

———❖———

Some weeks later, the sound of the doorbell made Michaela jump. The front door was thrown open to a beautiful blonde girl and her dark-haired companion. After Brigido let them in, he looked mystified as the two strangers embraced him warmly.

"Good morning," Michaela said as she rose from her chair.

"I am Tara Campbell, and this is my twin brother, Vic. We've come to visit you and would like that we can get to know you and—"

Brigido made for the door, but not before Vic touched his arm very gently. "Granddad, Tara and I dearly wanted to meet you and Grandma. We asked Aunty Marcia for your address. Please stay."

For a moment Brigido looked serious, as his eyes met Vic's

and then Tara's. He saw an uncanny resemblance between his grandchildren and their mother.

"The trouble is, I have allowed things to drift along for too long," Brigido said quietly, holding Vic's hand and upper arm. "It was wrong, so very wrong of me ..." His eyes became watery. "Please ... be patient with me. Your mother is a good woman ... like your grandma ... with solid values and a good sense of justice."

"Granddad." Tara met the gaze of his brimming eyes and watched him swallowing hard. "We're not here to rehash the past. You only get one chance to be a parent. You did what you thought was right – you cannot undo it now. Mum's favourite quote, by Oprah Winfrey, is this: 'Forgiveness is giving up the hope that the past will change.'"

Brigido flushed slightly and straightened his shoulders as he turned to face her. "I guess you're right. You have your mother's wisdom and courage. I've held myself back by past regrets. I'm not sure whether your mother would want to see me after all these years."

Tara stretched out her hand to include her grandmother. "Never mind. How about some tea? Vic's bought some jam doughnuts – *your* favourite too, I believe." She led her grandparents to the breakfast nook where she'd seen her grandmother seated earlier.

"Grand idea." Michaela smiled as she watched Vic arrange cups and side plates, while Tara organized the doughnuts on a platter. Brigido dabbed his eyes and looked from one to the other, absorbed in his own thoughts.

They're like their mother rolled into one, he thought. *What a fine job she's done in raising them. I'm so glad Michaela made the decision to reconcile. And I'm glad I agreed to stay for tea.*

CHAPTER 44

I t was a late November evening, when a sudden flurry of wind and a series of loud clattering, clangs, and bangs from outside disturbed Alexis's thoughts. She was startled and wondered whether Dante had returned and started clearing out the garage – he'd promised Tara and Vic that he'd free some space for parking when they came over Christmas. But he wouldn't be doing that at this time of the night, surely.

Then came another bang. "Good heavens!" she exclaimed, drawing back the kitchen curtain to look. "What's he doing in there? Must he be so noisy?" *This is so unlike Dante*, she was thinking. *He's usually very considerate and sensitive.*

On closer inspection, she realized that Dante had not returned but that the gates were swinging to and fro. She pulled on her jacket from the coat stand in the hall and opened the door. The wind was strong and icy cold when she stepped out to investigate.

Dante drove into the garage moments later. "Careful, honey," he said. "There's a storm brewing. What are you doing outside?" It was impossible to talk in the wind; she'd obviously not heard him.

"Thank God you're back," she said when she felt his strong arm around her shoulders. "I heard terrific noises, and I've just come out to find out where they're coming from. Use my torch," she said, handing it to him. "We can't be stumbling in the dark."

Together they walked briskly around their property and discovered much damage. Several tiles and pieces of glass lay smashed in the courtyard, garden, and pool area. As they rounded the corner, they noticed that the gale had ripped a number of downpipes to the ground. There were gaping holes in the roof and many loose tiles sliding down. The wind was growing stronger, and within seconds the shattering sounds recurred – more slates, roof tiles, and glass. It was treacherous!

Alexis's heart sank as she surveyed the debris around the property that she and Dante had chosen to begin their family. It held so many memories, and she couldn't imagine the length of time it would take to do repairs in this wintry weather. She was barely within reach of the front door when the rain came down, bringing thunder and lightning in its wake.

"After all the expenses we've just incurred, do we need all this, just weeks before Christmas?" she wailed. "The timing of these disasters is preposterous!"

"Alexis, get out of the rain!" Dante shouted. There are loose tiles on that roof that could slip down and hurt you. I don't want you landing in hospital. I'm securing the awnings so that the wind does not rip them apart. Don't wait for me – hurry up!" He battled to tie the ropes; he could barely see what he was doing. His hair and clothes were already soaked.

"Dante, we're in trouble, with all that rain," she said, rushing into the laundry. She ran up and down the stairs with containers, towels, and newspapers.

The phone rang. Dante contemplated ignoring it, but when the ringing persisted, he snatched up the handset. Although the caller was polite and friendly, he did not recognize the voice. Hoping it was the wrong number, so that he could hurry on and help Alexis, he took a chance by repeating the number of their landline.

"I'm sorry about your home; it's a pity the property developers had to choose your area."

He felt anxious about leaving Alexis by herself and wanted to get this call over with. He did not have a clue who that this person might be. She'd have to call back later, he thought.

"We have an emergency in our home, and I've got to help my wife – we have a huge problem! Sorry, I've got to go now!" But there was something about her tone that told him she had an important message.

On the other end, Michaela was not giving up. "It's just been announced on the news that Brighton has been earmarked for a new airport. We wondered whether you've decided on where you will live. You see, we haven't yet handed to you the title deeds to the house. And maybe this new development might be an ideal opportunity for you to relocate."

"Mrs Versini ... I mean Michaela ... uhh, Mum," Dante stumbled over his words. "I'm so sorry ... I'll have to get back to you on this. I need to help Alexis – she's on her own sorting out a problem on the top floor. Thanks for the news – I appreciate it. Let me have your number and we'll call back later."

Michaela rattled off the number, and Dante attempted to commit it to memory, deciding that he would not tell her about the flooding just yet. He'd only heard of but not yet met Alexis's parents.

As he put down the phone his heart thumped wildly. He had no idea how he would break *this* news to Alexis – she was so attached to their house and had not commented much about the family home she'd inherited. Questioning or pressuring her was not something he planned on doing. This was strictly her call; the twins shared his views on the matter.

Alexis had made use of the pool cover to protect the furniture and carpet in the guest room. Her quick thinking prevented serious rain damage, as she had cleverly placed large basins and buckets in each of the rooms with layers of newspaper beneath them. After hours of running up and down, replacing soaked newspapers and taking turns to empty containers, Dante and Alexis saved themselves from considerable indoor damage.

Dante, noticing Alexis's bare feet and damp clothes and hair, guessed that she was probably freezing and tired after all the rushing and fussing about. He ran a bath downstairs with her favourite oils and placed her towels on the heated towel rails. Her white bathrobe, woolly slippers, and snug pyjamas would be ideal, he thought, as he placed them in her spacious bathroom.

"Honey," he said. "You must be exhausted after all that rain beating down – thank God we've prevented major indoor damage. There's something you've missed – let me show you." He took her hand and led her to the bathroom to enjoy some respite after all the drama.

Dante was in his favourite armchair watching the news on telly when Alexis walked in looking cosy and more relaxed.

"Mmm, is that my favourite seafood pizza you've ordered?" she asked. "And what's this ... ahhh! Bonarda Frizzante to go with it. What a feast after all that fuss! Come along, Dante – aren't you hungry?"

He turned down the volume and enjoyed the takeaway with her. Occasionally he found her staring wordlessly at the walls, ceiling, and floor. He wondered whether she had any idea of what was in store for them. Just then he heard the word "Brighton" on TV, and he turned up the volume on the CNN Channel.

"Plans are underway for the airport to be built in time for the Commonwealth Games in two years' time. The Council has given the go-ahead for this project to be launched. Most of the residents have been informed, bar those in the northern region of the area. Families will be handsomely compensated for this land transfer."

Alexis gave way to the tears that had been threatening from the time she had encountered the damage to their house. She pushed the food away, leaned back on the sofa, and sobbed bitterly. Dante reached out his hand and smoothed Alexis's hair from her face.

"Have I not endured enough, Dante?" she sobbed. "How much more am I expected to take? I have forgiven my parents, my insensitive teachers, my tactless friends and neighbours. What have I done to deserve this?"

She shot to her feet and started throwing the scatter cushions around the room, picked them up again and again and continuing in this fashion until Dante rose and joined her. When she noticed him doing the same, she smiled and began throwing cushions at him, and he returned them. They ended up giggling like teenagers, until both of them collapsed in a heap, still laughing and out of breath.

"Dante," she said thoughtfully, "the question is, what did I do to deserve you?"

"Alexis, my dearest," he said caringly, "you need never *do* anything or *be* anyone. I love you for who you are – just *you*!"

"You deserve a medal for putting up with me ... I've been cranky, nasty, and wretchedly unjust."

"And I've had *my* share of faults," he said putting an arm around her shoulders. "You've taught me throughout our marriage that inner strength and contentment comes from living in hope."

"Dante," she said softly as fresh tears streamed down her cheeks. "Let's not talk about the house tonight. Let's ring the twins and invite them to spend the weekend with us. This is still their home, and it means a lot to them. By talking about it and including them in discussing other possibilities, this could be the best closure for them as well as us." She dabbed her cheeks as she thought of the effect that the eviction could have on them.

Dante held her close as he sensed her deep anguish and

sorrow. His own tears stung in his eyes, and he allowed them to flow freely.

"Alexis, God has a unique way of making his purpose known to us. Look what happened today. Our house was struck before we got the news. Nothing material or financial will replace the sentimental value of this home. You and the children are home for me, not a building."

She sat up and faced him. "I feel the same, Dante. All this," she said, pointing to the walls and furniture, "can be replaced, but you and the children mean far more to me than bricks and mortar. With you, *home* could be under a tree." She embraced him affectionately and listened to his breathing.

"Let's have some hot chocolate, shall we?" Dante said as he gently eased her away.

Alexis heard a slight tremor in his voice and gently drew him back to the sofa. "Talk to me, Dante," she said. "Tell me what you're feeling. You've been a rock throughout our marriage; allow me to hear you – what's happening for you?" She noticed his red-rimmed eyes and sensed that he was in pain.

Dante leaned back in the chair and wept, his body racked with sobs and gallant efforts to talk, but the words remained stuck in his throat. Alexis placed her head on his shoulder and her hand on his heart. She allowed him to pour out his pain, already thankful for the relief that this would bring. When his sobbing subsided, Alexis gently lifted her gaze to meet his.

"Alexis," he said softly. "You've received so many blessings in your life, in spite of the misery you went through as a child. Lady Tamar and Lord Victor presented you with a share of the Consani Village Hotel and the Manor, but you wanted us to build a home, and look what's become of it."

"Landing rights for air travel – that's what it will be. But we have a new home, Dante, refurbished and modernized to include our children and grandchildren. It's a gift I've despised, but God's asking me to humbly receive from those who have hurt me most – my parents."

CHAPTER 45

"Mum, Dad," Tara called. "We're here." She helped Vic carry in their luggage and waited for a response.

"Upstairs, honey!" Dante said. "Come to the spare room – we've something to show you."

"What happened?" Vic asked, his jaw dropping when he saw what it was. "How long have you known about this leak, Dad?" He took the bucket from his mother while he waited for them to explain.

"The recent storm," Dante said and studied their faces as he spoke. "It was very violent – seemed to hit the higher buildings in the area. Quite a few of the roof tiles have been damaged, and two of the patio doors are dangerously cracked." He walked down corridors, pointing out the areas that had been targeted that night.

"Dad, it looks like there's been an implosion – it's fortunate neither of you were injured. Your quick thinking has certainly diverted the flooding. These carpets and furniture have seen better days, I'd say. The ceilings are quite bad, but they could have been worse."

Tara became emotional. "Why didn't you call us, Dad? We heard the storm, but we didn't realize its intensity. We're not babies. Look what you've had to do on your own, and we were home playing stupid cards," she wailed.

Alexis had just cleared the room of the damp papers when she heard Tara weeping and her dad trying to explain and pacify her at the same time. She broke into the conversation. "Tara," she said, "remember how you thanked me and your dad for not judging you when you had a certain problem as a teenager? Can you remember? At least your dad and I were together that night. Parents are not meant to rely on their children for support and nurturing; they marry each other and turn to each other for

175

help – as Vic likes to put it: 'Even when you're sick of each other, poor with each other, and dead with each other.'"

Laughing through her tears, Tara said, "I know, Mum, but it's scary to think what could have happened. Imagine if we had come and just found the two of you here – dead and buried under rubble. It happens, Mum!" she said as fresh tears streamed down her face.

A wide grin spread across Vic's face when he spoke. "Tara, you remind me of Gran. She told us how she nearly missed the train and how she cried, wondering what would have happened had she missed it." He laughed louder as he recalled the story.

Tara joined in. "Yeah, and when the ticket inspector came, she realized her oyster card was in her suitcase, and then she cried because she was worried about what he could have said to her."

Alexis and Dante laughed too, but neither of them had heard those anecdotes before. Dante was very close to his mother, but she'd never told him this story.

"When did Gran tell you this, Tara?" Dante asked.

"Gran told us," Vic said. "Gran Michaela. Tara and I went to visit her and Granddad."

Alexis and Dante exchanged glances. This came as a huge surprise to them.

"Are you upset, Mum?" Tara asked sheepishly.

"Upset? Never! I'm proud of both of you," she exclaimed and embraced them warmly.

"Why are we standing in this makeshift shower?" asked Dante. "Let's make ourselves comfortable in the lounge. I want to hear the whole story. Alexis, you're not cooking today. Let's order Chinese and some more seafood pizzas – it's our favourite, isn't it?" He winked an eye at her and caught the cushion she threw at him teasingly.

Alexis watched her husband as he listened to their children talking animatedly about their maternal grandparents. A brand-new sense of tranquillity settled in her heart and being, as it dawned on her how much she had gained in life from the very adversity that life had thrown at her.

Tara was busy with the décor around of the house and was all but finished when shrieks of laughter at the front door interrupted her.

"What's all the excitement about?" she asked. "Oh wow! It's the Versini army! Make yourselves at home!" she said. "Tonight's only the planning meeting, right?"

"Yes," Cathy said as she admired their family's former home. "You've done wonders to this place since our last gathering! Whose handiwork is this? I can hardly wait for the celebration."

Alexis smiled proudly. "There's an artist in the family," she said. "We won't have to worry about décor or visit art galleries anymore." She placed an affectionate arm around her daughter. "This is our artist," she told them. Come and see the rest of the house – all credit to Tara, Vic, and Dante, while I've stood back in amazement at what's been done here. Come and see!"

Alexis's sisters made a tour of their former home, admiring the exquisite touch of luxury befitting the most deserving family member and heiress to this magnificent mansion.

CHAPTER 46

The next couple of months flew by. Vic and Tara met regularly with their maternal grandparents and shared with them their hopes and dreams. Vic had a special way with his grandfather and often called him by his first name – a habit that the elderly man took great pleasure in.

Brigido inquired about the purpose of two colleges on the same premises.

"Why do you run a boys' academy and your parents a girls' academy? Isn't that a bit sexist for an orchestra? I'd have thought that having a choir or band that was mixed would be far more balanced and enriching, and I think it'd create a healthier rapport among fellow students."

"Brigido, my man," Vic said. "I've never thought of that, but I think it's a splendid idea. I'm not sure whether Mum or Dad will agree, but I like the idea very much." He mused, "We'd be re-inventing the wheel. I can see us sharing our expertise, building healthy boy-girl relationships, and having less rivalry among the students." He queried, "Why haven't we met sooner, Brigido?"

Tara looked pensive. "It's not that you haven't thought about it, Vic," she said. "It was an unconscious decision that you took. Mum projected her prejudices towards boys by excluding them, and you did the same with girls. But now that you're aware of it, you can fix it!"

Brigido's eyes were watery, and he nodded thoughtfully. "I wasn't the best father to your mother and her sisters. I made horrible mistakes." He spluttered in his efforts to stifle his sobs. "Your mother's a strong woman. I was the head of the home, but I was a very weak one at that."

"Granddad," Tara said gently, "Mum's never spoken ill of

you – she's glad that we visit to spend time with you. Dad too; he wanted to hear some of the anecdotes that Gran told us about. You need to forgive yourself and move on. God does not hold our mistakes against us; we do that for ourselves." Tara washed his mug and switched on the kettle when she saw her granddad reaching for his handkerchief and dabbing his eyes.

"My daughters challenged me," he continued, "but I found ways and means of ignoring them. I was so angry with God for giving me another daughter. I reared your mother as a son until she stood up to me. Though still so young, she was courageous, courteous, and very assertive."

He acknowledged Tara's gentle touch on his hand when she placed a fresh mug of tea at his place.

"You're great kids, the pair of you," he said. "No wonder you're twins. You have twin souls."

———❋———

Alexis and Dante agreed that joining forces would save them time, energy, personnel, and finances. Vic was willing to step down as head of department as long as his parents created a post in the school for him. They agreed to discuss this at the following board meeting so that the parent body and students would have a say in the plans before any final decisions were made.

For weeks after this initial conversation, Alexis and Dante's quietness intensified as the problems around this possible unification multiplied. Vic began to wonder if he had made a mistake in proposing this to his parents. The tension in the staffroom grew worse, and cliques formed – something he'd never experienced before. He wished he knew how to handle the conflict.

His visit to his granddad was the only chance he had to sound off without feeling judged or unduly criticized. He told of the tension, backbiting, and unpleasantness in the school and how he regretted making the proposal.

"My dear Vic," Brigido said as he gently wiped his grandson's cheek with the back of his hand. "Change is never easy. Your colleagues are afraid of change, and that's what you need to deal with first. You need to prepare people for change. One day you'll prepare your children for a new sibling in the family. Even toddlers are jealous when a new baby is born. You don't change for the sake of it. It's a process – a slow process – and it takes time. You're forcing the rosebuds to open here. Learn to wait. That's what hope is about."

"Granddad, you're a wise man. I'm so glad I've met you. I feel a few milligrams lighter. I wish I had your wisdom. I'd have done this long ago." Vic whipped out his mobile as it bleeped a message. "I've got to go. We've an important meeting with the parents this evening, Mum's just informing me. Please God, no more drama tonight."

When Vic arrived, his parents and colleagues had already gathered to discuss how they would deal with questions. His Dad invited the personnel from both academies to join hands in silence and stand as one before the parents, irrespective of the outcome of the meeting. His request was amicably accepted.

Dante opened the meeting by asking parents to express their feelings when their sons and daughters had asked permission to drop some of their academic subjects to study music. They were to share this in pairs or small groups and to report back to the large group. Their sharing brought lightness to the atmosphere, as they acknowledged their initial scepticism.

"Change takes time," Alexis said in her address to the parents. "We have no intention of making any structural changes in the school. Our intention is to begin with a mixed choir and take it slowly from there. Come to our first concert at the end of the year, and then give us feedback at our next meeting." She saw an elderly gentleman raise his hand at the back of the room, but because time was against them, she was reluctant to invite another speaker.

There was a shuffling sound in the hall, and when she looked around, Alexis saw Vic and the personnel from both academies on the stage behind her. Vic was tasked with doing the closing address.

"Ladies and gentlemen," he said. "I don't have anything else to add to what has already been said and shared here tonight. My colleagues and I wish to pledge our commitment tonight. We promise to take it one step at a time, in collaboration with you and your children. Could you promise your allegiance to walk with us in faith – not ahead or behind but *beside* us? Let us join hands as we pray "The Lord's Prayer" and ask God to be our shepherd in this new venture. We're not to walk beside him, but behind him."

The elderly gentleman at the back of the room still had his hand raised. Alexis's mobile bleeped, and she slipped into the corridor to answer it. Tara was holding the fort at home while they were away. The family get-together was due to begin within two hours, and she still had a host of things to do. Alexis checked with Dante and then slipped away to help Tara.

Vic smiled mischievously at the gentleman and invited him to speak. Everyone turned to face the friendly looking man.

"My dear people," he said in a strong voice. "My generation was of the old school: we kept our boys and girls separate, and what happened to us? Many of us had not learnt to relate to the opposite sex. The only female persons we knew were our wives. While that is right and very healthy, we did not understand our daughters, our granddaughters, and our nieces, and it was vice versa for the women. Now here's a chance to change all that. What are we waiting for? I want to walk beside this school and behind my God, but I challenge this parent body to offer support in kind. I have a daughter and a grandson on the staff in this school and granddaughters who are students here. I am pledging an undisclosed amount as my gift to them. What about you? Will you place an offer on the table?"

The atmosphere was electric, as parents and teachers applauded, whistled, and gave thumbs-up signs to the elderly gentleman. When asked his name, his answer was very simple: "Mr Victor Campbell knows me; that's enough for now. Good night!" And he left the hall.

CHAPTER 47

ante drove home feeling excited about the celebration to be held in their home. Everything was meant to be a surprise. Tara and Vic seemed to have something up their sleeves, though he didn't dare to ask. He was interested in the elderly gentleman, whom Vic seemingly knew. He must remember to find out who this man's daughter was – he wished Vic would tell him.

Marcia, Maria, Ancilla, Terése, Zoë, and Cathy looked radiant in their evening wear, as did their husbands and daughters. The caterers were doing a fine job with the cooking, and everything was going according to plan. Vic and Tara were tasked with hosting the celebration, as their parents stood in line with the Versini siblings. Dante's parents and sisters were also in attendance.

Alexis was glowing in her royal-blue shimmery evening dress; her hair was in an up style with the front strands trailing across her face. Dante stood beside her and winked at her as they stood facing the front door, waiting for their guests of honour. Eventually the doorbell rang, and Tara answered it. Lady Tamar and Lord Victor entered, and everyone applauded. Alexis knew that they celebrated their birthdays on the same day, but she was unsure of the date and how old they were. Nobody sang to them, so she wondered when the guests of honour would be acknowledged.

A voice announced, "Alexis Campbell, please take your place at the ice sculpture!"

"What's going on?" she asked Dante. "I haven't prepared a speech for Lady Tamar and Lord Victor. You could have said something, Dante. Come and stand with me," she pleaded. Dante simply smiled at her, kissed her hands lightly, and left her to stand on her own.

Alexis looked around, wondering who it was that had spoken and what this was all about. As she stepped forward, a drumroll sounded, and everyone applauded.

"Starting today," that same voice announced, "every year, this day will be marked as Versini Reunion Day; our thanks to Alexis Versini-Campbell."

Dante's younger sister Bridget handed Alexis a giant key. The voice continued, "You have brought this family together by playing a key role. We commend you for your contribution to music and your sterling work among the poorest in the community."

Bridget's twin sister, Celine, presented Alexis with a registered envelope for the Alexis Academy of Music – *from DD Versini*. The envelope was to remain sealed and its contents undisclosed.

Cass and Bianca stepped forward carrying a large table with a variety of kitchenware, as the same voice declared, "For a friend with a heart of gold – a mentor, teacher, coach, landlady, and non-biological sister. Thank you for giving us a taste of family life through your hospitality and welcoming spirit."

Lady Tamar and Lord Victor stood on either side of Alexis as the voice reverberated in the room: "Thanks, Alexis, for your example of forgiveness, your magnanimity, and your willingness to learn and grow. You've been an inspiration. I was known in my day as a tough counsellor with a title. Victor and I'd prefer it if everyone dropped our titles as from today. The key you received earlier is the key to the Three Sisters Manor, a family heritage, and a very special oasis, of which we'd like you to take charge."

Tara discreetly removed the lapel microphone from Lady Tamar; her voice echoed in every part of the house: "Mum, Vic and I grew up very close because of you – not the perfect you, but the struggling and in-pain mother that you once were." Tara's tears streamed, but she continued heroically. "You learnt to listen, and this made the world of difference to our household. You taught us to love, forgive, reconcile, and give people a chance to trust and to care for themselves and others. Of all people, Mum, you had enough cause to become bitter and resentful, but you saw its effects and you turned your life around. Thanks for doing that, Mum." She stepped away and passed the microphone to her brother. Vic continued.

"My darling mother," Vic started. "Dad gave us permission to be creative. The portrait that I'm about to unveil is our tribute to you. Beneath, it reads *Et disrumpetur spiritus unum*, meaning 'The Courage of One'.

"We've chosen to adorn our main wall with you, Mum, because by your example in life, you've taught us that one person can make a difference in a home, a family, a community, and the world at large. Thanks, Mum, for being that one." He embraced her warmly and passed her hand to his father.

"Alexis," Dante said, "thank you for being my wife, my friend, my confidante, and the mother of our children. You have blessed my life every day, and I remain enriched by it." He handed her a pearl bracelet and helped her slip it onto her wrist. "This is to remind you of the nacre of life and how your inner beauty continues to emerge to make you into a priceless work of art."

Alexis was about to respond to every speaker, when she heard a familiar voice. "Alexis!" She remained glued to the spot, her heart racing. Was this really happening, or was it a dream? She felt her palms perspiring, while her legs and feet were like jelly. She tried, but her voice was gone. She waited, stared ahead of her, and saw a mirror reflection of herself: a motionless, speechless individual with outstretched arms.

"Alexis!"

Alexis had originally been led to understand that there was to be a special celebration. Meanwhile, she had learnt that the family had agreed to celebrate her unifying role in the family. She breathed deeply, and lifting her feet that felt like lead, she moved forward.

This was her moment of triumph; her hidden childhood fear had dissipated. She knew she could do this and dearly wanted it with all her heart. Continuing with slow steps forward, she spontaneously opened her arms, recognized the clear dark eyes and the quivering smile. With a few long strides, she was back in his arms – the arms of her beloved father.

"Daddy," she said, "I've come home. We're all home. It's good to see you! I've missed you so much!"

"Alexandra … my sweet daughter … I am so sorry, so very sorry. Thank you for coming home. I think this is the best remedy for my heart." He lifted her and swung her around as he used to do when she was little.

Alexis, overcome with emotion, placed her head affectionately on his chest as they danced around the room, while Dante played their personal favourite, John Denver's "Perhaps Love".

As if on cue, Alexis and her father sang the closing lines in a harmonious duet:

And in those times of trouble
When you are most alone,
The memory of love
Will bring you home.

A NOTE BY THE AUTHOR

The Courage of One unfolds the truth about every human being – that what we become in life is what we choose to become.

The common belief that our lives go awry because of what others do to us is a crippling concept, because neither our circumstances in life nor the attitudes of others have the power to block us from living life to the fullest.

With the right mental attitude and self-confidence, anyone can change the course of life to make it beautiful and worth living. For a highly motivated person with a positive outlook, no goal is too big to achieve and no obstacle too insurmountable to overcome.

In the ebb and flow of her life, Alexis touches many lives, while her children grow up taking definite paths of their own making. Their lives surprisingly bring them to a point where history merges into one dance and unfolds events and experiences, woven in a colourful tapestry, that bring forgiveness, inner strength, integrity, serenity, love, and enduring peace.

Through her heroic efforts and faith, Alexis reclaims her inner power and allows the light to shine in the darkness of her world, where self-defeating thoughts are unleashed. She convincingly reminds us that psycho-spiritual growth is not only meant for a few but is everyone's birthright.

Printed in the United States
By Bookmasters